THE

FIRST WIFE'S

SECRET

A NOVEL

ADDISON MOORE

Edited by Paige Maroney Smith

Cover Design: Gaffey Media

Published by Hollis Thatcher Press, Ltd.

Books by Addison Moore

Mystery

Little Girl Lost

The First Wife's Secret

Cozy Mystery

Cutie Pies and Deadly Lies (Murder in the Mix 1)

Bobbing for Bodies (Murder in the Mix 2)

Pumpkin Spice Sacrifice (Murder in the Mix 3)

Gingerbread and Deadly Dread (Murder in the Mix 4)

Seven-Layer Slayer (Murder in the Mix 5)

Red Velvet Vengeance (Murder in the Mix 6)

Bloodbaths and Banana Cake (Murder in the Mix 7)

New York Cheesecake Chaos (Murder in the Mix 8)

Lethal Lemon Bars (Murder in the Mix 9)

Romantic Suspense

A Sublime Casualty

Romance

Just add Mistletoe

Low Down and Dirty (Low Down & Dirty 1)

Dirty Disaster (Low Down & Dirty 2)

Dirty Deeds Low (Down & Dirty 3)

Naughty by Nature

Beautiful Oblivion (Lake Loveless 1)

Beautiful Illusions (Lake Loveless 2)

Beautiful Elixir (Lake Loveless 3)

Beautiful Deception (Lake Loveless 4)

Someone to Love (Someone to Love 1)

Someone Like You (Someone to Love 2)

Someone For Me (Someone to Love 3)

Burning Through Gravity (Burning Through Gravity 1)

A Thousand Starry Nights (Burning Through Gravity 2)

Fire in an Amber Sky (Burning Through Gravity 3)

The Solitude of Passion

Celestra Forever After (Celestra Forever After 1)

The Dragon and the Rose (Celestra Forever After 2)

The Serpentine Butterfly (Celestra Forever After 3)

Crown of Ashes (Celestra Forever After 4)

Throne of Fire (Celestra Forever After 5)

Perfect Love (A Celestra Novella)

Young Adult Romance

Ethereal (Celestra Series Book 1)

Tremble (Celestra Series Book 2)

Burn (Celestra Series Book 3)

Wicked (Celestra Series Book 4)

Vex (Celestra Series Book 5)

Expel (Celestra Series Book 6)

Toxic Part One (Celestra Series Book 7)

Toxic Part Two (Celestra Series Book 8)

Elysian (Celestra Series Book 9)

Ethereal Knights (Celestra Knights)

Season of the Witch (A Celestra Novella)

Ephemeral (The Countenance Trilogy 1)

Evanescent (The Countenance Trilogy 2)

Entropy (The Countenance Trilogy 3)

Melt With You (A Totally '80s Romance)

Tainted Love (A Totally '80s Romance 2)

Hold Me Now (A Totally '80s Romance 3)

Heat not the furnace for your foe so hot that it do singe yourself.

—*Henry VIII*, William Shakespeare

One

To: Parents of Richard E. Moss Elementary School

From: ItsmeTessaPTA@moss.org

Subject: Monte Carlo Night Fundraiser

Heads-up! I'm going out on a limb to say this will be our most successful fundraiser ever. There will be appetizers, pizza, and booze! Yes, we scored the approval of the board to have beer, wine, and cocktails on school grounds for the night. Not a single person under twenty-one will be allowed. All guests will be ticketed and carded at the door. Don't forget to be social. This is a great opportunity to get to know other parents and staff as well. What better way to get to know your child's teacher than while sharing a glass of rosé? Please monitor and limit your drinking. No sloppy drunks or puking. And remember above all else, spend lots of money and have a great time! All proceeds go to upgrading classroom materials and equipment. Please mind your designated drivers. Volunteers from the PTA are willing to take your keys and provide transportation if needed. Stay safe and sane. Let's make this the best night ever!

Ree

They say you can hear your name even when whispered at impossibly low decibels. And I would swear on my life that I heard mine. Not the nickname I had come to adopt as my formal moniker, but my full name, the one I hadn't used or heard since that painful time in my life. I buried that name in the past along with who I was. But I heard it, I would swear on my mother's grave if she had one. And how I wish she did.

I follow that sound, that demonic whisper as I spastically take in the vicinity.

A spray of crimson dots the linoleum flooring, a sloppy dotted line that leads right to the darkened hall next to the janitorial supplies, and I give a hard grunt as if it will be me cleaning up the mess. It will—that's what all the grunting is about. I've signed up for the cleanup committee because that's what you do when you're new to the PTA board, new in town, a mid-year move no less. It's what you do when you desperately want to fit in and have all of the obnoxious mommies in their preppy little mommy cliques like you—at least a little bit. You sign up for the grunt work, no pun intended, and the gruntiest grunt work of the night falls to sweeping up the facility with your husband—because a good wife volunteers her presumed good husband. And now that some bastard has spray-painted the floors, Bram and I will have to scrub for hours getting this stain off the—

The high gloss sheen catches my eye, and I bend over and swipe my finger through the sprinkling of cardinal. My God, it's not paint at all. I think... I think it's blood.

"911, what's your emergency?"

"Oh my God, I've found a body! It's a woman. It's a very beautiful woman, and she's dead. She's dead, dead, dead!"

Six minutes earlier...

"Monte Carlo Night is ingenious, really," I say to Bram, my handsome devil of a husband. *Devil* being a word

I would never use openly to describe him. He's an angel when you get down to it, but that dark wavy hair, those sage green eyes—he's comely in an obvious way. He's one of those men you see on the streets with a plain Jane and you ask yourself, what's a good-looking guy like that doing with a girl like her? Only in this equation I'm the infamous *her*. Okay, so I'm not quite as plain as a pancake, but I'm not strutting the runway in Milan either. And Bram, well, he's to die for—another dark analogy I would never *ever* breathe out loud.

Bram spins on his heel over the slick gymnasium floor of Richard E. Moss Elementary School—grades K through six. That was another major draw to this locale, the great school system. If Bram and I are about anything, we're all about our children. Some might say unnaturally so, but if you dug past our hygienic exterior, if you peeled back the layers of who we were and what we've been through, you would say, yes, they are fine parents and with very good reason. Bram and I are helicopter parents squared. There will be nothing but the best of the best for our Lilly and Jack. We already know how much there is to lose.

"The cake is chocolate sin." He nods as he lifts his

plate to me.

"No thank you. I gave at the pasta bar." It's true. I inhaled enough carbs to fuel me with enough energy to lap the planet twice if need be. My punishment would be no dessert. My mother and her enormous girth bounces through my mind, and I happily bounce her right back out. My mother has haunted the recesses of my mind for the better part of the last ten years. It's been that long since I've seen her, and as much as I wish she were dead, she's still rolling around the planet according to my sister. Lena and I escaped her clutches, but sometimes when you run from someone, a monster so scary you wish never existed, you need to keep slight tabs on the demon just to be sure you're running in the right direction.

But Bram and I are all through running. We moved to Percy Bay, a small seaside community in mid-coastal Maine. It's just a short drive to Belfast where Bram's brother, Mason, lives. His mother is in Connecticut. His father is out of the picture, so at least he has a sibling in close proximity, the same way I do. Bram and Mace are close, but Lena and I are practically the same person, and that's why she's moved into the house directly across the street from ours, a small rental that's working out perfectly for her. We're hopeful this will be our final move, if not our longest stay. Bram just underwent a legal name change as well as going through the drama and trauma of having his name altered on his dental degrees. I took his new name, as did the kids—our kids, Lilly and Jack. We are the Woods—not a far cry from Woodley, but the kids were accustomed to the sound of it, so Woods it is. The irony being our new moniker wasn't chosen based on the logical leap from Peter's—*Bram's*—formal last name—but for the phrase we often whispered to one another in the night. *We are not out of the woods.*

Peter Woodley and Aubree Van Lullen have stepped out of the proverbial woods as Bram—yes, after his favorite horror author Bram Stoker—and Ree Woods. And here we are, hiding in plain sight, unafraid, unmoved by the flinching glance of a stranger. We have started from scratch and will do so again and again until life sings the right narrative.

Bram wraps his arm around my waist and brushes his lips to mine, a move that still makes my cheeks flush with heat. "They're coming in hot, six o'clock."

I turn my head in time to see the mighty three, Tessa Holmes, Astrid Montenegro, and Bridget Geraldi. Tessa is the head of the parent-teacher association, a volunteer position you would think she trained years for at Harvard. Tessa is congenial, someone everyone naturally gravitates toward, with an open heart-shaped face and overeager smile. Her skin is perpetually bright pink as if she's trying too hard on a cellular level, and her eyes bulge with bullfroggish glee when she looks at you. They're the exact entrancing shade as Bram's, and I suppose that makes me like her just a little bit more. Her husband is a plumber and "very much in demand in this leaky copper-lined town"— her words, not mine.

Astrid is an impossibly tall blonde with one of those stylish mermaid bobs, squinty smoky eyes that perpetually drift toward my husband, and she's in the habit of wearing low-cut tops that bare the chest she purchased for Christmas last year. She has a buyer for her clothes, all of which she models to no end on Instagram, which amuses and entertains just about everyone because she's "oh-so hip". She seems to be well-liked by the masses, although, honestly, I can't figure out why. She hasn't been the most welcoming to me. Her husband is an investment banker, and they're rumored to have massive amounts of real estate holdings in the area.

Bridget is a two-dimensional perpetual scowler who let me know in no uncertain terms the day we met that she couldn't really "hang out with me" at school events because she had her own friends. I couldn't help but be a bit amused by the adolescent remark. Apparently, she was in a violent car accident a few years back with her brother. He suffered head trauma and hasn't been the same since. You would think something like that would pull someone out of a junior high mentality, but she stands firm in protecting her clique from me.

"Bram"—Astrid strokes my husband's sleeve with her blood red nails—"I believe you owe me a thank you." She gives a sly wink accompanied with a dolphin-like giggle. "I'm personally responsible for the candy bar—aka cavity central." More braying and the rest of us join in as we pick up on the joke.

Bram just signed on as the third full-time dentist at Smile Wide General Dentistry in downtown Percy.

"Well, thank you." He gives a gracious bow. "While I

certainly appreciate the business, I feel obligated to bring a tub full of toothbrushes to the next school function that might have more than ten grams of sugar per capita."

Another round of warm laughter ensues.

Tessa steps in toward Bram with her mousy blond hair. A white lace shawl thrown over a pink tank top and jeans is an ultra-dressy look for her. "Miles and Chuck are at the blackjack table. This is a great night to meet the other dads. Just tell 'em Tess and Ass sent ya!" She snickers into her jewel-toned cocktail as she brings it to her lips.

I take a moment to glance to Astrid who's rolling her eyes. She's no fan of her posterior-based nickname, but from Tessa it's practically a term of endearment.

Astrid also happens to be my neighbor two houses down on Strawberry Lane. It was the name of the street that enchanted Bram and me more than the actual house we purchased, an old split-level mid-century Spanish without an honest upgrade, sans the kitchen—thank God for small granite-based mercies—the rest of the house is still cursed with the single-paned windows. And don't get me started on the wobbly slider doors—all installed backwards by the inept builder—someone could easily slip a stick into the well of the flashing and lock us inside our own home. Both showers leak, the kitchen sink has zero water pressure, there's a nonsensical pit in the backyard that you could break a leg in—the list goes on and on. But we bought in the very best neighborhood, a sought-after neighborhood accustomed to bidding wars. We came in all cash with the money that Bram received as a payout from the death of his wife and children. It was blood money he called it. But in the end, he decided we needed it and practicality won out.

"Blackjack." Bram bounces a quick kiss off my lips. "I promise I won't bet the farm." He gives a sly wink and makes the girls swoon ten times harder before ditching us for the dazzling display of dealers and scantily clad women from the catering staff strutting around in adorable ruby red bustiers and thin black chokers.

My stomach stirs with jealousy.

A very faint, insecure part of me is worried that Bram will wake up one day and see that he's made an egregious error and leave me for someone newer and shinier with a lot less baggage. But, in truth, it was our baggage that drew us together, moth to the wicked flame.

Astrid offers a spontaneous applause. "Blackjack, roulette, poker, craps, gin rummy— we have it all. Best fundraiser we've ever had at Richard E. Moss. And I should know. I've been here for—"

"Eight years"—Tessa finishes for her and winks my way. "She has a six-year age gap between her boys. Two different baby daddies," she whispers mischievously, lifting her glass my way.

"God, Tess." Astrid yanks Bridget to her. "You can be so juvenile when you drink. One of these days, I'm going to murder you in your sleep."

Bridget gives a husky chuckle. "Maybe you should both watch your backs." She looks to me as she says it, no smile.

My God, some people never leave high school. It's as if her brain were still imprisoned somewhere between home ec and an arduous gym class where they make you run the mile uphill both ways—and a part of me thinks she'd deserve it. She's been subhuman to me from hello.

"Ignore them." Tessa steps in close, that wide face of hers only seems to expand unnaturally as she leans in, the hot breath of scotch steaming my skin. "Ass is just jealous that your husband is way hotter than hers. She actually had the balls to ask me how much a dentist earns. She feels threatened because you moved into the same neighborhood. She's used to being the richest, and the prettiest, but you've upturned her on both counts." She gives my ribs a quick pinch and belts out a cheerful guffaw.

My cheeks flush at the thought of outshining Ms. Percy Bay herself, but I'd gladly steal both titles if they were true.

"And what about Bridget?" Her name comes out with disdain on my part, my own vodka tonic boozy breath joining the party. In truth, everyone under this seemingly innocent gym roof has a high-octane blood count right about now. We voted in the liquor once we heard that patrons were apt to spend up to three times more than expected if they had a healthy helping of alcohol running through their veins. Astrid pointed out that people were more apt to get laid that way, too, ensuring a good time would be had by all. "She's so stoically quiet it's as if she's hiding something." I doubt it. She's not sinister or dark enough in the slightest, just your run-of-the-mill vapid phone-to-ear moron who wears heels for no good reason. If giving dirty looks were an Olympic feat, she could medal. Not to mention she still thinks cliques and popularity scales are a thing.

"Oh, Bridge knows where all the bodies are buried." Tessa lifts her chin as if driving home the point, and a shiver runs through me.

Not an analogy I want flaunted in a social circle I was desperately trying to inject myself into.

A moment stumps by as Tessa's eyes remain locked on mine, and I wonder if she's trying to tell me something. That familiar burn in the pit of my stomach starts in, and I have to get out of here, must get some air.

"I think I'm going to run to the little girls' room." I start to head that way, and Tessa pulls me back by the elbow.

Her prairie green eyes shine like quarters in the sun. "We're all looking forward to the kids' party on Sunday. Please let me know if I can bring anything."

A flood of relief washes over me. The normalcy I long for is still within reach.

"Just yourselves, and, of course, your kids. Lilly and

Jack are over the moon. Bram's rented a bounce house, and I've got enough cake on order to ensure Smile Wide will have a steady stream of clients for the next year straight." We share a quick laugh and I'm on my way, breezing through the crowd of glammed-up soccer moms and their paunch-bellied companions, who actually look mildly pleased to be at the quasi-cool school function. It's a win for the PTA, a win for the dismal fiscal state of the slush fund we're looking to enrich, and a win for the newly-minted Woods—who might not be out of the woods just yet.

The faint whisper of my name, my full name arrests me. So faint, threadbare, but I heard it. I follow the sound with caution as I head for the back and an arresting spray of sanguine liquid catches my eye. The cleanup committee, the spray paint, it all cycles through my mind in two seconds flat. I bend over and slip my fingers through the greasy mess and sniff it—copper scented. I know this smell, this ruby red sin of a feel—blood indeed. I take a few careful steps into the darkened corridor, and that's when I see her, brunette, pretty, eyes wide open, a wire cinching her neck to the size of a dime, her left hand mutilated, and I scream.

It seems Bram and I are never really out of the woods.

———————— ♦ ♦ ♦ ————————

A body, a corpse, right there at Richard E. Moss Elementary, and, of course, I had to find her. My bad luck knows no end. The image of the woman stains my brain and I can't escape her. She lies over my eyes like a film, an overlay that demands I see my own children through her body.

Sunday shows up like an axe-wielding intruder, a threat to my sanity, as I swing around the house in an unreasonable dress with a full skirt like some 1950s housewife, with my turquoise leather flats, my hair curled ridiculously as if I were going to prom circa 1988. I've dusted and cleaned, buffed and polished until the house gleams like a river stone.

Lena has been hostage in the kitchen for the better part of a day and a half, making sure the side dishes are just so, cutting the crusts off mounds of peanut butter and jelly sandwiches. Cooking is her forte, not mine, and it's times like this I'm grateful for it.

Bram has left to pick up a stack of cheese pizzas, and at the last minute I asked him to throw in a few buckets of fried chicken. Lena has made her signature Chinese chicken salad in a bowl the size of a bathtub. She assures me that all the mothers will devour it before begging for the recipe, and I'm guessing she's right.

I'm new to the kiddie party scene. Lena is, too. Lena, my older sister by two years, has been dutifully by my side since birth, my only companion for so long, my only friend. Our mother shaved our heads before we could properly walk or talk and kept us glued to wheelchairs we didn't need, feeding us a pittance of a diet to keep us morbidly thin, sheltering us from the sun to keep us sinfully pale, and that is how she made a living. Donations from churches and her various places of part-time employment proved a nice subsidy for us for a long time. She claimed we were homeschooled, very ill, too ill to venture outside and have a normal life, but she paraded us around when she needed to. But it was Lena and I who taught each other to read, to learn every basic skill in life we could get our hands on. Our father (which I'm assuming were two different men) was nothing more than an enigma to us. Once, my mother mentioned she had met him in a bar, and I figured we were the products of one-night stands. A darker thought had come along, though, and I wondered if my mother was turning tricks at the time. She herself was virtually abandoned. She had one sister who lived nearby, and neither of them had been successful at life.

But, in truth, we were Cordelia Van Lullen's favorite crutches, living in a bubble of her own making, turning a dollar faster than she ever could off those minimum wage jobs she held. We were a curious burden to her at first, quickly followed by an amusement, and then a very serious source of income. Eventually, Lena and I figured out we were just fine—not one damned thing wrong with our well-functioning bodies, so we moved in with my aunt in high school, but not before we suffered abject humiliation and were run out of town, our pictures plastered all over the news, national media, our mother arrested for a time. Both Lena and I tried our hand at junior college. We were avid readers, self-taught mostly, but as fate and our mother's selfish agenda would have it, we were not scholastically inclined. Lena works for a local caterer, and I write children's chapter books in my spare time that I'm hoping to sell one day.

That body. It floats to my mind at all the wrong times—in the shower, on the toilet, making love to Bram. I still see her startled eyes, bulging and crimson. Her pink tongue fat between her lips. And the blood. My God, my stomach turns just thinking about it, and I quickly usher the corpse away.

Instead, I force my gaze to flit out the window. The clouds are dark and fat on this late March afternoon, and the bounce house is steadily wobbling from side to side. Lilly and Jack scream to unholy levels from inside it, screaming with glee, of course. I know all of their whispers and whimpers, and these are of the joyful variety.

I pass the hall, and my eye catches on those framed black and white prints of Isla and Henry, doppelgangers of Lilly and Jack. Those mops of dark heads, those smiling Irish eyes—

it's all so very eerie.

Lilly is eight today, the exact age Isla and Henry were the day they drowned in the lake. Isla and Henry are, *were*,

Bram's children with his first wife, Simone.

We have never kept them a secret, never shut them out of our children's lives. They are ever-present in the hall just outside our bedroom, an entire wall devoted like a shrine to their young, vibrant lives cut short far too soon. A day at the lake that turned tragic. The sitter tended to her jilted heart by way of weeping into her phone while the kids swam out too far and got sucked under.

But Bram swears the lake was glassy, both kids strong swimmers. His wife, an editor at the local paper in their upstate New York life, quit her job and spent her remaining days buried among the couch cushions. Then another tragedy struck, a break-in, a bludgeoning. Simone was gone just like the kids, and, of course, everyone thought Bram had done it. He was already hung in the court of public opinion by the time they caught the real perpetrator, a man by the name of Erwin Wilson, a homeless man prone to bad decisions, breaking and entering while in the midst of a psychotic episode. A burglary gone wrong. A rape gone wrong. Everything had gone wrong for the Woodleys.

Two dead children. One dead wife. Bram lost his

practice and was run out of town. He couldn't sell or rent the house, and it sat empty for years until last fall. A builder offered full asking price. He's going to raze it and put in a duplex. Fair enough. We really don't care.

The doorbell rings, and Lena shouts that she's too busy to get it, so I sail downstairs, trying to ignore the fact dog hair has amassed to each step. As much as I love our Husky, Dawson, he is a shedding machine. Twice a year it snows Dawson. You can't have a meal without a dog hair in it. My mother hated the creatures, and that made me all the more certain I would always have one.

I swing the front door open, an old wooden carved wonder the previous owner—original owner at that—had shipped from Mexico. It's inlaid with an intricate floral design, and one day (soon hopefully) when we remodel, I plan on using the door as a base for a custom desk. It has character, and what better place to plot and ponder my own characters than this old door that I'm sure has more than a few haunted stories to tell.

"Packages." A cheery UPS man squints out a smile as he slips in two large cardboard rectangles into the foyer before whisking back to his truck.

"Oh, thank God," I moan. "The decorations are finally here!" I shout to Lena as I kick them past the entry enough to close the door. As much as I adore Dawson, he is a runner, and I swear the day he sails out of our lives and bounds down the street will be the last we ever see of him. Not really, but I'm a lousy dogcatcher and even lousier at slapping missing posters to every tree in town. We have him chipped, and I'm hoping that's enough to keep the shelter he finally gets turned into from adopting him out behind our backs.

I muscle open the heavier box of the two. My God, did I put in an order for concrete? I pull back the lid and reveal three bright red Dutch ovens nesting in one another, the lids wrapped neatly in paper by their sides. My heart sinks for two reasons: I didn't order these, and I happen to appreciate how pricey these are. Lena has been after me to get my hands on one for ages.

I'm sure they were meant for somebody else, most likely Astrid down the street, but a horrible part of me wants to keep them.

The kids scream with laughter, pulling me out of my Dutch oven induced trance, and I quickly move onto the second box. I need to throw some party hats about and pull out the happy birthday banners as quick as my limbs allow. We look incredibly ill-prepared to host the entire second and third grade classes from Richard E. Moss Elementary. Lilly and Jack's birthdays are two days off and one year apart, so we've always celebrated at the same time. So far, no complaints. I run my finger along the seam of the lighter box and feel the burn over my skin as it gives, and once I peer inside, my stomach drops again. Not a sign of anything remotely happily cartoonish. Instead, it's just a pile of old composition notebooks, bloated used ones at that, some paperbacks, and an emerald tin coffee can at the bottom. I pull it forward, and it's full of old costume jewelry, a few gold rings, a silver necklace, and a pair of pearl earrings that may or may not be real. I slip the lid back on and pull open one of the composition notebooks. It's a journal.

"Huh." I rock back on my heel, taking a moment to slip through a few pages. It dates back to 2008, the penmanship neat and heavily slanted, pleasantly legible, yet not flowery, clearly a woman's. The color of her pen varies every so many pages from black to blue, to red to green, no particular pattern, just whatever she could reach for that night I suppose. Then I see it. My eyes snag on an all too familiar name, first Henry, then Isla. I quickly spot Peter in the mix, and a rush of bile inches to the back of my throat.

Went to the grocery store. Henry pitched a fit and wanted a bouncing ball. Why the hell do they put those in the middle of the aisle? There was no way around it. I bought two. Henry chose red and Isla bought a purple marbled wonder. Peter was not happy with my spontaneous purchases. I'd like to see him get out of the supermarket alive.

"What in the hell?" Something enlivens in me. My skin prickles with heat, and my adrenaline spikes. I flip to the next page and read mid-paragraph in haste: *the veins in his neck bulged when I told him. I hate that Peter suffers from such silent rage. It's because of all of that bullshit with his mother. I don't need a therapist to tell me—*

"Ree?" Lena calls from the kitchen, and I slap the book shut. "Where's the olive oil? I'm going to whip up some garlic bread. Don't tell me you're out. We just bought a gallon at Costco!"

"Right pantry, on the floor." Shit. I quickly move the heavy box full of iron pots into the guest closet, and as I bend over to pick up the box full of journals, I spot a yellow envelope taped to the inside flap. I quickly pull it forward and free the letter.

Found the pans in the drawer under the stove. A lot of people forget about that space. Thought you might be missing these. And the rest of the stuff was culled from the basement.

Tim Bergman

Tim Bergman. That name rings familiar. He's the contractor who bought Bram's old house. These are Bram's things. I glance to the box filled with the bloated books. Simone's personal journals.

My blood runs cold. I doubt Bram knows about those journals. He would never have left them to rot. These are his memories, too painful as they might be.

His car pulls into the driveway, and without thinking, I whisk the small box upstairs and bury it deep in the back of the walk-in closet, throwing a pile of sweaters over it for good measure, just below the gun safe. This closet has become a treasure trove of secrets. But if ever there was a day for keeping secrets, this is it. For sure I'm not souring Bram's mood this afternoon. I'll tell him about the delivery tonight or even tomorrow once we've come down from our birthday high. I flick off the lights and head downstairs, feeling a bit guilty as if I've just taken Simone, Isla, and Henry off the invite list.

Bram comes at me with a kiss, warm and juicy, the promise of things to come. He's in a cheerful mood, the only mood I've ever known from him, so that insert in Simone's journal resounds like a gong in my ear.

Bram and I help Lena set up the last of the buffet, spreading it over the dining room table, paper plates at the ready. I can't help but cast a wistful smile at the walls. When we moved in, they were stark white and I insisted on painting them red, something cozy, a nice holiday feel I said at the time. It was a post-Christmas haze that had inspired it, and now that even Valentine's Day is behind us, the color just feels wrong, offensive even. It's as if the walls are angry, the entire house were wishing to be rid of us.

The clock strikes one and Bram, Lena, and I freeze a moment like three lonely children standing in the cafeteria on the first day of school just hoping the cool kids will ask us to sit with them. In reality, we're wondering if the cool kids will show at all. And sure enough, they do like a flood. The glut of second and third graders run through the house and straight for the bounce house out back as if it were magnetically pulling them into its gravity.

A handful of mothers linger in the backyard whispering amongst themselves in groups of two and three. The rest of them asked what time the pick up was and took off for child-free pastures. A part of me marvels at the fact they've entrusted us with their most prized possessions. If they only knew who they were dealing with, they would have certainly thought twice, or most likely not come at all. But most of the PTA is present and accounted for, lingering among the crepe myrtles out back, so I suppose there is a small comfort in that. Bridget arrived with her nose buried in her oversized phone. The sparkly pink case looks as if it were an accessory for one of Lilly's Barbies, and yet some small shallow part of me envied the way it caught the light.

The doorbell rings and in pops Tessa with her down-to-earth sense of style, cut-off jeans as if to usher in the warmer weather and a pink sweatshirt that reads *Moss Dolphins*, expounding the fact that she's forever the cheerleader.

"Hello, Woods family!" She gushes, her eyes swollen with that never-ending glee she seems to propagate, and I can't help but love her. Tessa's brand of cheerfulness is a contagion and one I'm happy to contract. We exchange a brief embrace, and she lunges for Bram as well.

"My God, you have quite the house!" She takes in the red walls with an exaggerated inspection, and my body heats as if I could feel her judging me.

"It was a post-Christmas thing," I say stupidly, and Bram shakes his head at me as if to stave me off from going there. He's already heard this a dozen times. Reiterating my regrets is a nasty habit I've yet to rid myself of. For as long as I can remember, I've been prone to apologizing for my decisions, for my very existence, and I'm sure all the people my mother bilked money from would appreciate the latter. "I'm not sure I'll keep it, though—the color. It's really hideous now that I've lived with it for a bit."

I hear Lena groan audibly and give me the finger

behind Tessa's back. I know that Lena thinks I'm kissing her ass, and perhaps she's right, but my nerves are jangled from the body, from that box that landed at my feet this afternoon, and all I want is to fit in for once. Lena leaves the room, and I take a breath.

"I'll be repainting it soon. Brown, I'm thinking."

"Brown?" Bram muses. "We might have to take it to a committee. Lilly and Jack would probably vote for—"

"Green with purple polka dots," I finish for him, and his left brow hikes with amusement. With Bram everything is an inside joke. We take a bit of perverse pleasure in knowing why it's so important we meld seamlessly into our new world. We overcame our extraordinary odds, fought like hell, and now we are a normal, such a horribly normal and boring family. A dentist and a housewife. We love to sell it as much as we love the illusion.

"No way!" Tessa protests while fanning her arms over the startling color. "I love the red. It has to stay." Her theatrics alone are worthy of leaving it be for a lifetime. "Isn't that right?" She looks past me as Bridget joins us.

Bridget's eyes flit to Bram, her tongue does a quick revolution over her lips, a subconscious primal cry for him to impregnate her. I've convinced myself that on a fundamental level, women of childbearing years would love to sleep with my husband. Bram must sense this, too, because he steps in close and slips his arm around my waist. He's been claimed, and he's not looking to explore his options.

"Red? Really?" Bridget's fingers tap over her lips as she beats her fingernails against her teeth. "They say red is a color that insecure people use to disguise the fact they have no power." Her lips twitch just shy of a smile as she flits those dark, soulless eyes my way. "But you bought it that way, right? I mean, you didn't deliberately choose the color."

The doorbell rings, and I make a move for it without hesitating. For a brief moment, I'm wishing it were Bridget I had discovered with her neck the size of a thimble. The police still haven't released any information on the *body* as they so coldly referred to the poor girl I had the misfortune to discover.

I swing the door open to find a pert Amazonian blonde, skintight jeans, crop top, just-ate-the-canary grin on her face, Astrid. Tucked in her arm is an enormous chicken, a majestic beast whose plumage actually stuns with its long onyx-colored feathers. Its beady eyes and frenetic head jabs, letting me know it doesn't want to be here anymore than I do at the moment. I spot Astrid's kids running around through the back gate, most likely not wanting any association with the lunatic before me.

"You've brought a guest," I say in my brightest voice, widening the door to let her know undeniably that poultry is allowed. I'm the cool mom who lets this shit fly. Can't wait to see Dawson's reaction. I'm sure he'll be spitting out feathers for a week.

No sooner does Astrid strut her tiny frame into the foyer than Tessa bounds over and embraces both the bird and the bitch. "You've brought Rocky!" She does a little dance, cooing and oohing at the frightened beast, and it gives an alarmed flapping of the wings.

"Oh, hush you." Astrid tightens her grip over the poor thing as she looks to Bram. Something cinches in me when she does it. Don't think it's gone unnoticed that each time we're together she pretends I'm a part of the furniture and treats my husband like a single father. "I hope you don't mind the early wake-up call. I'm trying to get rid of the rooster, honest I am, but I can't seem to place him in a decent home. I've got a flock of fourteen right now and more baby chicks on the way. My animals are my family. The kids know I love my feathered friends best." She belts out an awkward guffaw.

Bram and I exchange a sharp look. So she's the culprit with the damn birds who love to rouse us as soon as the sun hits the horizon. We gift a knowing nod to one another, always on the same page.

See? I want to say to those around us all too eager to drop their panties for my husband. We are a united front. Our bond is unbreakable.

"We don't mind a bit." Bram does an odd little hop backwards. He has never been a good liar. "I think I'd better ring the bell and get those kids eating before the food goes cold. You ladies, too. Chop, chop," he chides before disappearing, and both Bridget and Astrid give a schoolgirl giggle.

"So, Ree." Astrid leans in with her elf-like features zooming in a little too close for my liking, her pecking friend, jutting its own head out toward me as if pleading for assistance. "Rumor has it, you touched the corpse. You

41

tried to revive her yourself. That's quite heroic. Was it someone you knew?"

I inch back a bit. "No. Actually, I don't know who she was. But I can assure you I never tried to revive her. I felt the floor. I thought it was paint, but it wasn't. It was—"

Astrid pushes me to the side in a violent fit as she takes a step toward the dining room. "What the hell?" Her eyes are agog at the streams of miniature hands all snapping up food off the buffet table at once. The bounce house sits deflated out back, slouching over itself like a tired old man. I'm guessing unplugging it was Bram's sneaky way to get the kids to take a break and eat. I spot him outside, cornered by a petite redhead, her hand petting his arm every other second as if comforting him.

"Don't worry. We have enough food to feed an army," I insist. "In fact, if you want to get started yourselves, I can have the Chinese chicken salad brought to the living room. *Lena!*" I give a shout to my sister but am met with silence on that front. Lena's sequestered herself in the kitchen, and it doesn't look as if she's coming out.

"Holy shit." Astrid staggers into the dining room as if I've chopped up a body and fed it to the miniature masses.

Tessa's eyes grow wild as she inspects the scene. "Crap." She stomps on over, and both Bridget and I follow like a couple of lost puppies.

Astrid yanks a peanut butter and jelly sandwich right out of some poor boy's mouth and screams at the children to get back outside.

"Are you trying to kill us?" she riots while nailing me in the face with the unfinished sandwich. "Bridget, get out there and take that shit away from them. Hose down their hands. Nobody touches anything. I want everyone the hell off the property in five." Her eyes meet with mine, furious and dangerous. "You do not feed a group of children peanut butter under any fucking circumstance. Do you hear me? One sniff of that shit can send anyone even remotely allergic straight to the ER. I am damned glad I brought my EpiPen."

Tessa steps in. "Okay, calm down. We've got the kids taken care of. Brian across the street is a pediatrician." She looks to me and nods, as clearly that bit of info was for me. "I'll have him give everyone the once-over. And I'm sorry, Ree. She's right. We've got a hell of a lot of allergies this year, and we'll be lucky if we don't end up with another

corpse on our hands today. My God, it would be a child."
She looks to the ceiling. "You don't want that. You do not
want to know how it feels to have a child's corpse haunting
you."

"No, of course not." My heart throbs in my throat,
and my veins pulse with heated adrenaline. I've sweated
right through my clothes, and the air feels steely against
my skin. I'm ripe with embarrassment that poor Lena has
to witness the event, even if she is cowering in the corner,
snickering away, saving all of her best lines for later, and
I'm sure I will hear them. But Tessa is wrong. I know
exactly how it feels to have a child's corpse haunting you.
In fact, I know what it feels like to have two.

Astrid spots the bucket full of chicken legs spiking out
of their cylinder-shaped home as if taunting her, and she
seizes, causing her ridiculous bird to let out an ear-splitting
squawk. She lets out an arduous cry herself before
sneering at me and stalking out to the back.

"I'd better help get the kids to safety." Tessa helps
her usher the children single file through the rear gate
swiftly as if the backyard were suddenly on fire.

I head out, only to meet with Bram, his arms folded

tightly, his pale green eyes penetrating me with a mixture of disappointment and heartbreak. The veins in his neck bulge, a silent rage just the way Simone had pegged him, and I quickly sweep his poor dead wife out of my mind. We are trying too hard. I shake my head at him, and he shrugs back.

We plug in the bounce house and join the kids. Lilly and Jack laugh and scream. They don't even notice the other kids are missing. Lena comes in and sits in the corner, enjoying the ride we afford her. Bram holds my hand, pulls me in, and steals a kiss. He whispers *I love you* straight into my ear, and it almost feels as if it's going to be all right.

That night I scan my emails before bedtime. Twelve new messages. Almost all of them far kinder than expected. **Sorry things turned out that way! I'm sure that will never happen again. I hope the kids will be at Willy's party next week—we're having an insect zoo! Ricky and Ann had a good time anyway!**

Tessa sent one that read **Don't tell anyone, but I still buy peanut butter. Next time you're in my neck of the woods, pop over and we'll share a sandwich in secret.**

I can't help but give a dull smile.

One from Bridget: **You have snack on Tuesday in Lilly's classroom. Don't be an asshole.**

Nothing from Astrid. She's as red as my wall, I'm sure. I've never seen so much rage in a person, not since my mother. I'm sure she's through with me.

And just as I'm about to abandon my phone for the night, another email pops up as if to contest the theory.

Twokidcircus@bex.org: **Woven jacquard drapes in the bedroom are considered a crime in some places. The red bedspread looks about as tired as you. I did wonder, though. What is in your closet?**

The world stops spinning a moment as Simone and that box that contains her private journals race through my mind. I bolt off the bed and head into my closet, leaving the dim light from the bathroom to illuminate my sweaters still heaped over the cardboard. I peer in to find the contents untouched and cover them back up again. Someone had the audacity to invite themselves upstairs, to judge my curtains, my bedding, my closet, and its contents. They were making a point.

I'm starting to think our move to Percy was a mistake.

I'm starting to think that no matter where Bram and I go, we will never escape the past, never escape the bodies, finding fresh ones along the way.

Bram and those veins bulging along the sides of his neck come back to me. My husband lost in his silent rage. It seems inescapable at this point.

My heart drums into my ears all night long.

I don't catch a wink of sleep.

Two

Bram

They say you remember the first time you lay eyes on the love of your life forever—deep down, there is an intrinsic connection that indelibly etches the moment into your psyche.

I stroke my wife's honey-blond hair while she sleeps beside me and marvel at how soft it is, how soft she is, how perfect in every single way. The early morning light baptizes her with its luminescent fire and her body glows like a flame. I remember the first time I laid eyes on my wife. I was seated in a bar where I had all but taken up residency. The Boar's Tavern was a seedy kind of a bar where you could lose your sanity and your soul if you wanted, and I was indeed on the verge of losing the latter. I had already lost the former. It was one of those nights that I was busy with the task of taking inventory on whether or not I needed to hang around on this planet for another day, and Ree walked in, smiled my way as if we had a date, and just like that, something switched on inside of me and I knew. I knew that Ree was the one. Her toothy smile was so brilliant it almost knocked me right out of my seat. That's what I have etched in the recesses of my mind. She gave me a brand new reason to live right at that moment.

"What's your name?" she asked after landing on the stool next to me. She cited she was waiting for a friend, but that friend never did show. I remember thinking this woman is so bold. First of all, to set foot in this dive with that face and that body, and second of all, to crack the ice without any pretense. But I came with pretense, guns blazing.

My mind wandered for a moment. It was close to Halloween, and the place was laden with cheap cardboard cutouts of witches and ghosts, but it was the cartoon vampire with his spiked fangs that caught my eye.

"Bram." And right then, I spoke my first lie to the woman who would be my wife. It's important to note that the very first word out of my mouth to Ree was in fact a lie. Straight to the deceit—no chaser. And just as I was about to ask for her name, reciprocate her boldness right back into her lap, I opted for something far bolder. "My name is actually Peter." My own smile dissipated. There was nothing funny or even fun about being Peter anymore. Peter was about to step off a bridge. Peter was a downer just about every way you sliced him, and a majority of the nation had enjoyed doing that for the better half of a year.

"Peter?" Her brows hiked a notch, and I couldn't help but note that it only magnified her beauty. She had a clean, open face, clear amber eyes that mesmerized me right off the bat. A face you might see on the cover of a health magazine for women. Her lips were slicked with a blush of color, but everything about her screamed natural beauty. It made me think of Simone, her thick layers of creamy foundation, the caked-on powder that sank into the creases. Grocery store bleached hair. Everything about Simone was hard, unyielding, and my stomach knotted up for having the thought. You shouldn't think bad things about dead people. You should especially never think bad things about your wife who was brutally murdered less than nine months ago. It is a bad, bad thing to harbor hatred in your heart for the mother of your two dead children. They say a tragedy like that has the power to tear apart a marriage, but the floor to ours had rotted out long before that.

"My name is Aubree." She held out a small pale hand, and I glanced to it as if I didn't understand the mechanics of what she was asking. "You can call me Ree."

"You must be a reporter." I gave a quick shake. I will admit, there was a twinge of relief to have solved this puzzle, and to think for a moment I believed she had wandered in here, this fabulous woman, and things might have actually started looking up for me once again. "No offense, but I proverbially gave at the office." In reality, I gave up my office. My thriving dental practice hit the shitter once word circulated that I had taken a hammer to my wife's face. Of course, I did no such thing, but the jury of public opinion didn't see it that way, and what they chose to believe quickly became my reality. No, not many patients visited the office after Isla and Henry had drowned. There was a dark cloud that hovered over my once blooming medical practice—even I could see it, feel it touch it, taste it. But after Simone was killed so very brutally, not even a mouse dared traipse across my office floors. A majority of my staff quit, citing every excuse under the sun, and the last few stragglers I had I ended up placing in my competitors' offices. There were still a small handful of people who believed me, who would testify under a grand jury if I asked them to on my behalf.

"I'm sorry." She shook her head. "I'm not following. I'm not a reporter. I work at the DMV part-time." Her lips twitched, cherry red, and I couldn't help but dip my gaze to them every now and again, wondering what they might taste like. I shook the thought out of my head. I'd stepped out of my mind if I thought this woman, this beautiful healthy young work of art would ever want anything to do with me once I spilled my truths like a jar of marbles. A hardened part of me, the one calloused by life, said *Don't breathe another word. Get her loaded. Take her home. Get some relief for once.* But I didn't have it in me. "I just finished up at the community college." She wrinkled her nose, and something about the sweet action assured me she just might be blissfully clueless as to who I was, what I had done, and the things that I had been accused of doing as well. It's a clusterfuck of truths and lies, all stewing in a bubbling brew, and not even I could see where the forgery began and the truth ended.

"Can I buy you a drink?" Something in the air between us loosened, and she laughed, exposing twin rows of perfectly straight teeth, not a filling in sight and, believe me, I would have spotted them. Simone's teeth were made of chalk. We used to joke about them. She said she married me for the free dental care and we would share a laugh. We knew better, of course. Simone married me for reasons unknown, but the regrets on both our parts kept coming. I don't think there was a human on the planet Simone could have married that would have made her happy. Her favorite catch phrase was *I can do anything better than you*. She sang that taunt, and it became her mantra. Our every move had become a competition. A part of me wondered if in that moment, when she realized she was going to die, if she felt some sense of relief that it would all be done with, the arduous race she related life to. There was evidence of a struggle before it was over for her. If Simone knew how to do anything, she could put up a fight. And she would not fight fair, but that wouldn't matter. What mattered was she was going to win and she would. There was never any disputing the fact.

I think back to the day I met Simone. Fresh out of college at a friend's graduation party to be exact. I didn't stand a chance.

"A drink? Of course." Those telling brows of hers dipped with concern, and when the bartender took our orders, a scotch for me, a virgin daiquiri for her, I saw where the concern truly lay. She didn't drink. Another red flag spiraled up, but I refused to heed it. That had always been my problem with women. I was too waylaid by their beauty, their intellect, to heed any harbingers that might be thrust my way. One of the first things Simone told me was that she always got her way. I thought it was cute. Something to tuck away for later. What I should have done was dive straight into the swimming pool we were lingering near—drowned myself and saved everyone a heck of a lot of heartache. But when you meet someone new, you truly don't know how to gauge the future. Those tremors in your stomach could just as easily be butterflies as they could be a warning of deadly things to come.

Ree told me about her time at the junior college, her ambition to write children's books. How she passed all of her classes with flying colors but had no plans to further

her education.

"That whole classroom setting wasn't for me." She bit the cherry off the stem and moaned, her shoulder touching mine a moment, and my insides pulled tight with lust, something that I hadn't felt in years. "I didn't go to traditional school."

"Homeschooled?" I was intrigued.

Her eyes flitted to the ceiling. "Something like that. My mother"—she sighed and took a breath—"she needed my sister and me at home." Her shoulders turned in toward me, and the smile faded from her face. "I hope you won't think less of me for what I'm about to tell you." And just like that, I knew I wanted to spend the rest of my life with her, protecting her from whatever seeming regret would pour from her lips.

Simone slapped through me like a car jackknifing through the freeway of my mind. They say you'll remember the first time you laid eyes on the love of your life forever—that deep down, there is an intrinsic connection that indelibly etches that moment into your psyche. The day I laid eyes on Simone, I was more than halfway drunk, my good senses already abandoned, and with Simone they never did recover.

The room around me takes shape as I sink back into reality. I take in Ree's vanilla-scented hair before slipping downstairs to make her favorite breakfast, buckwheat pancakes with a cup of fresh coffee. Of course, I'll be a hero in the kids' eyes. They love pancakes as much as their mother. Isla and Henry did, too. A forlorn smile twitches on my lips as they come to mind. As horrible as it sounds, I've trained myself not to look directly at their pictures as I head out of the bedroom. Too sad. Too morbid. Too furious of a way to start off the day or end it. Each time I look into my sweet angels' eyes, I hear them cry out to me from the grave. *Daddy, why weren't you there to save us? Why couldn't you protect us?*

My bare feet hit the cool travertine as I breeze into the kitchen. As soon as I spot the maleficence, my heart stops, the breath is knocked right out of me. Bearing their footprint over the top of the stove sits three blood red cast iron pots, the best in cookware. I should know. I just may have bought them. My legs carry me numbly over to them, and I run my finger over the lid. Could these be one in the same? If Ree asked for them, I was going to suggest she pick another color. I would never want the reminder. Simone loved them.

"I bet you recognize those," Ree calls light and cheery from behind, and I force the hint of a smile to grace my face.

"I do. How did they get here?"

Ree swoops in and wraps her arms around me. "Builder found them in the bottom drawer of the stove and shipped them. Wasn't that nice of him?"

The knot in my stomach loosens just a bit.

"Yes. Very nice."

"You don't mind if I keep them, do you? These things cost a fortune, and I've been dying to give them a try."

Dying. I can't help but frown at that one.

"Absolutely. Keep them. They're yours." The knot ratchets right back up again. "Did he send anything else?"

Her mouth opens and closes. Ree gets that *I love you* and *I'm sorry for you* look in her eyes that she wears every now and again for me.

"No. Nothing else." She winces. "I'm sorry."

"Don't apologize." I pull her in close and dance her in a slow circle until those pots are glaring at me, red-faced and angry as if they were personifying their last owner. "You have nothing to be sorry for."

I do.

Three

Ree

I lied.

I lied to my beautiful, sweet husband because I couldn't bear to see the pain in his eyes. I'm lying again. God, I'm so ashamed. I drove the kids to school this morning, ran over to Lena's to taste her blueberry scones—fresh from the oven. Lord have mercy, they were to die for. To die for, which brings me back to Simone. Those journals. I've spent the last few days pouring over the first one—how shameful that the anticipation is building in me to get to the end as if her life were some cheesy dime store novel. But, in truth, it reads much better than that. I'm addicted to her conversational tone, her easy wit—which has never been easy for me. It seems to solidify the fact that she was miles more intelligent than I could ever hope to be. I've always felt insecure around Bram in that respect, like a schoolgirl infatuated with her teacher, secretly knowing they'd never be intellectual equals. And I'm ashamed to admit that reading Simone's diary entries makes me feel a hint of jealousy of who she was and what she might have shared with my husband. I get that he was her husband first. Bram hardly ever speaks about her, and the few times I've prodded him, he's brushed the topic off as if it were still too hot, too visceral to broach. And I understand that completely. It was a nightmare within a nightmare to have the things unfold in his life the way they did.

I make a quick cup of coffee and head upstairs, casting a quick side-glance at Isla and Henry, their colorless faces staring back at me accusingly. I had offered to put up a picture of Simone as well, but that was a hard no from Bram. Understandable, completely. It's too painful, the grief too disabling. Lena thinks he's done it out of respect for me, and if that's the case, I do appreciate it. But I would never say that. It sounds so petty, it frightens me to think I could be so shallow. She's dead, and he's mine at this moment. There's no cat fighting over him. He belongs to both of us, and that's just the way it goes.

I land the coffee on the nightstand and pull another

journal from Simone's box of treasures. I've graduated to the next one, second to the last, and I'm gripped as if it were a heart-stopping thriller. It's sickening, really. Dead wife porn at its best—not in the porny way, but you get it. There is a sick, voyeuristic pleasure I'm deriving from these that only highlights the fact I'm certifiable, and with a mother like mine, this is no surprise.

I hop onto the bed, Bram's side, and feel a twinge of guilt, so I shimmy my way to the right until I fall into my own familiar divot. Bram and I have decided to live frugally, so a new mattress isn't even on the list. I sigh as I spot my coffee an entire lifetime away and snuggle into the pillows as if cuddling up with my favorite book.

January 16th

The kids are back at school—YAY! I actually cleared out the last of the Christmas crap but left up the mistletoe. I'll be sure to point it out to Peter once he gets home. He's been a bit stingy with his kisses lately, so I'll have to prime him, getting him back in the running for best kisser of the year. Speaking of which, new year, new me! I've renewed my membership at the gym. Come June, I'll have that bikini bod back in shape, and all the boys—I'm looking at you

Pete—will come a running! Crap. Just remembered I need to bake cupcakes for Isla's class tomorrow. Over and out!

Peter is a great kisser—I mean, Bram. And yet, he's never been stingy with me. I wonder if that's his way of making it up to her? He'll be the best version of himself now because he can't go back in time. It makes my heart ache ten times harder for him.

February 21st

My, how time flies when you're having fun! The stomach flu has invaded. The shits and giggles are quite literal around here. Peter says it's all my fault because I refused to vaccinate our tiny brood. Well, Mr. High and Mighty, you could have taken a damned day off and done it yourself. But, in truth, I probably would have hidden the kids from him. Do you know what they put in those things? No thank you.

Huh. I don't take the kids to get those either. The first time it came up, Bram stared at me as if I had just taken the kids and drowned them in the tub. Okay, poor analogy. See? Not that intelligent, after all. He looked angry, determined to let me know how he felt without words. *Strong, silent type*, Lena said when she met him. Her next assessment was: *scary*. Anyway, I completely side with Simone on this one.

February 26th

All is clear, and we survived! The weather is warm, and it feels like an early spring! I'm dancing on air because Peter and I are trying again! TRYING! Can you believe it?

My heart palpitates right into my throat. My God, they were trying for a baby? Bram never mentioned it.

I'm ovulating, so you can imagine the sexual insanity that's ensued for the last two blissful days. Peter came home for lunch, came again, and then went back. Ha! See what I did there? I'm feeling fun and flirty, so you'll have to excuse me. There is no better time in one's life than the season in which you and your spouse are equally smitten. And we are certainly there. I love him. My God, I love him so much. Sometimes I sit back and look at my perfect family and think how did I ever get so lucky? It almost makes me forget. Almost. Sometimes I think I've forgotten, and then stupidly I step backwards like I did just now and I remember. God help me. How will I ever forget?

Forget? Forget what? I speed read my way through the entire month of March and April and nothing, no hint of what she might have needed to so desperately forget. It didn't happen though, the baby. She had her period right on time both months. Her disappointment was cloying like a rag soaked in chloroform, forcing you to feel its effects even if you didn't want to. Smothering you in grief.

May 8th

Kelly arrived, Grant's niece from work. She's here early for the summer, and I've hired her to help watch the kids while I get some work done. Just when I think I'm done with freelancing, another "brilliant" story bursts into my mind—usually at two in the morning or when I'm deep in my bath with no pen in sight. But I digress. Kelly will watch the babes while I sit nearby and tap away on my keyboard. Besides, it's always fun to surprise Peter with my funny money paychecks. It's a splash of feminism in my Father Knows Best *world, and we both laugh at how paltry it is, in a fun way. It makes Peter feel all that much more like the provider he is, and in a way, it validates me, too. I've always been an attention whore. Peter knows it best.*

A writer. I bite down over my lip and contemplate this. How did I not know this? I didn't even bother to make the writer-editor connection. Maybe because I thought she wasn't at the paper for long. I'm certainly a writer. Yes, a writer of children's books certainly counts. I guess I had more than just Bram in common with Simone. But seeing Kelly's name emblazoned in black and white set a chill running through me. I already know this is the beginning of the end. It was Kelly who was at the lake with them that afternoon when the children drowned.

My phone burps, and I jolt as if it had the power to electrocute me from across the room. My heart wallops to life as my adrenaline soars, and I army crawl over the bed to reach it and accidentally knock over my coffee right onto the pricey sheepskin slippers I bought Bram for Christmas.

"Shit." I sling my legs over the side of the bed, and the journal slaps into the brown puddle. "No, no, no." I'm quick to wipe it off on the comforter before burying the book back into my closet, entombing it for another time.

I check my phone quickly just in case it's a message from the school, and my limbs solidify for a moment. It's an email from Twokidcircus@bex.org, the same person who sent that creepy email the disastrous day of the children's party. A snoop on the loose in my house.

Although in her defense—and I can deduce it's a woman because Bram was the only male at the party, but evidently not the only one with balls. They did after all traipse on up to my bedroom—but then the bathroom downstairs could have been occupied. Nevertheless, I had a lookie-loo in my bedroom that day, and they weren't shy about letting me know.

I click in.

Have you considered how rude it is to leave your curtains open at night? The entire neighborhood can see right inside. Your children fighting in their bedroom, your husband padding around shirtless—and, my God, those abs—that ratty red T-shirt you wear like it's a part of you. Please mind your manners.

A spike of adrenaline riots through me. My ears pulsate with a heartbeat of their own. I'm hot with rage. All I see is red.

That night, once the sun goes down, I make it a point to seal all the curtains shut with nary a seam exposing us to roving eyes. Bram is set to leave for a convention early in the morning, so there's no point in worrying him about it. This will all blow over. Whoever the hell she is can suck off because I refuse to entertain her level of crazy. There's no way I'm going to answer them.

Instead, I crawl into bed with my husband and his infamous abs. Bram and I make love sweetly at first, then with a fury. I bring all of my fire, my pent-up tension to the game, and it's a win for the both of us.

"I love you," he whispers hot into my ear as his body tenses over mine, and I clamp around him as if I were holding on for dear life. Bram and I vowed not to have any secrets between us, and holding onto those journals, those nasty emails, it feels as if I've severed a Godly covenant.

He'll be back day after next. I'll divulge every last detail when he gets home. My stomach churns at the thought, and it makes me wonder if I can finish the rest of the journals before then. I'd hate for Bram to take them away in a heated rage. It's the only time I've ever seen him show any uncontrolled outward emotion, the times he talks about Simone. It's all still too raw. Yes, even nine years later. I know how he feels. I still shake with rage when I think of my mother.

Those emails felt like a trigger, an unholy harbinger singing in the night. Like a comet burning up through the atmosphere that you need to squint to see on a dark, cold night. I cannot ignore the wickedness that's hurtling this way.

But I don't fall asleep soundly afterwards the way Bram does. Instead, I hug my pillow, and my thoughts drift to dark places, those secret places I vowed to never venture to again. And a part of me dares to think—maybe, just maybe, she's behind it.

———— • ◆ • ————

Bram doesn't wake me before he leaves, and depressingly enough I rouse to an empty space next to me, already cold, the warmth of his body long since dissipated. I shuttle the kids off to school, and none of the mothers in the drop-off lane even bother to give me the finger. I've become a social pariah once again, and, believe me, it wasn't for a lack of trying. My mother used to say the world would never love my sister and me, not the way she did. That we were hers until the end of time. But make no mistake about it. My mother never loved us. We were her playthings, to be controlled, manipulated, hers to keep or discard as she pleased.

I take the left onto Main Street and give a dreamy sigh. In truth, when Bram and I were scouting locations to set down roots, Percy Bay met and surpassed our needs and expectations. The ocean view from the main thoroughfares was a plus, the white powdered beaches we envisioned spending copious amounts of time on were major, the stellar school system had it in the bag for us, but for me an added perk was the small-town feel, the fact it indeed had a Main Street. It felt as if we were dropping ourselves into a Hallmark movie, the ones where every problem is quickly ironed out and love trumps all as the camera pans away. And yet here I am on the aforementioned fairytale-like street, the behemoth Atlantic looking murky and dark on the horizon, ready to discuss the latest information Lena has on the murder investigation from Monte Carlo Night.

I pull into a space right next to Lena's Suburban. Lena is the only person I know who doesn't have children, and yet her lifestyle demands an enormous vehicle. She does most of the deliveries for the Blue Chandelier Catering Service. She's also the manager here at the Blue

Chandelier, a low-key coffee shop that also serves up oversized portioned treats. It's my favorite place to come and unwind, and I love it that much more because it's quickly become Lena's baby.

When we moved here, it was the first place she applied, and, of course, they loved her. I head on in and soak in the heavenly scent of coffee. It's the first thing that hits you right before you're overcome with the ethereal nature of the ambiance. There's a large outdoor patio out back that delivers an expansive ocean view. It's always packed. You can never even hope to get a seat there. Every stay-at-home mom has turned this into her hub. It's the go-to place to have coffee, and the writers seem to have taken a liking to it as well. I can certainly see why. The mood is romantic in a tragic way, and they play Enya on a loop. The inside, however, is just as scenic, with the entire ceiling covered in ornate chandeliers in every hue of its namesake color. The floors are dark gray wooden-patterned porcelain tiles with the hint of silver sparkles to them. The walls are covered with navy shiplap, and there are wreaths made of lavender flowers just about everywhere you look. It's not your typical greasy spoon, and the décor is something out of a movie. I give a quick look around for Lena, and my eyes snag on a couple of all too familiar women, my least favorite cock handler and the forever hippie—Astrid and Bridget. Astrid spots me, and they cease their conversation to take a moment to glare my way.

"Here you are." Lena comes at me with a contrived embrace, coupled with steaming hot coffee in both hands, as she ushers me along to a table near the front, far enough from the bitter mommy brigade so they can't hear our conversation and yet not out of their line of vision. Lena was never one to run from a problem.

I can't help but frown a bit at my sister. Her eyes are heavily drawn in with black kohl, a look that both works for her and against her. Sure, it makes her pale green eyes pop, but it also makes her look like a thirty-year-old Goth gone wrong.

"What's this about the killer?"

She wrinkles her nose as she leans in tight. "Not the killer. They've finally identified the body."

I suck in a quick breath. "The girl!" I hated referring to her as *the body*. It's too generic. I have never understood the way someone is a beloved person one moment, a corpse the next. It erases every humanistic thing and reduces them to a phylum that doesn't even exist. You are less than an animal, relegated to something akin to morbid furniture.

"Her name was Erika Melon. She was from Manhattan. Her pimp helped identify her."

"I bet he did, and I bet he did it! What was she doing all the way in Percy? We're not exactly an L train from Times Square."

She averts her eyes at my weak attempt at New York humor. "They don't know. There are whispers of forensic evidence, but other than that, they have nothing. No leads, no motive, no nothing." Her eyes narrow in on me the way they do when she's good and pissed. "Just you, my sweet sister." Her plain nails drum against the marble table.

"I'm no lead, and I'm no suspect. The police questioned me that night and haven't been back. Thank goodness." I can't help but sneak a glance over my shoulder, only to meet up with Bridget's dark soulless eyes and I shudder without meaning to. "I have to tell you something," I practically mouth the words to my sister, and her hot breath heats the space between us. I pull up my phone and read off the emails I've received from that loon.

"Holy shit." She gives a long blink. "Who do you think did it?"

"I don't know. It could be anyone. We might not have had the world's longest party, but we had an army of angry mothers filling every orifice."

She grunts over at Astrid and Bridget just as they break out into an obnoxious cackle. "I bet it's one of those bitches." Lena has a dead look about her in general. She's stunning in an I-just-crawled-out-of-a-casket-way, but by and large it creeps women out. Men seem to love her, so there's that.

"I thought so, too, but the more I analyzed that day, the more I'm certain they were both downstairs the entire time."

"Not true. I let the brunette bitch in. You opened the cocky gate."

I bite down on my bottom lip so hard I taste the salty brine of my own blood. "I think maybe she sent them." I tick my head out the window, indicating yet another infamous *she*, and Lena's eyes enlarge a notch. It's a visceral reaction, but then, my mother only seems capable of eliciting those in anybody.

"No." She shakes her head aggressively. "Don't say her name. Don't you call that demon into existence. There is no way in hell she's capable of doing any of that, and you know it."

"She's capable." Tears moisten my eyes, and I'm quick to blink them away.

Last we saw of our mother, we were running for the car, arms full of clothes, of books. We had meant to escape while she was away at the store, but she forgot her purse and came back in half the time we had predicted. She was furious, livid. Our mother is a morbidly obese woman, with a tuft of black hair that rises over her head a good six inches. She was as insane to look at as she was on the inside, and yet for so many years we had bought into everything she was selling, namely us. And we were weak on that getaway day, our limbs rubbery from years of sitting, our lungs stretched to capacity as we tried to dive into our aunt's Ford Tempo.

Exactly one year after the great escape, our aunt was found in a motel room, an empty pill bottle by her side, facedown in the bathtub. My theory has always been that my mother had drowned her first. Of course, it was ruled a suicide. My mother was impervious to law enforcement and any other governing bodies that rule the land. She has had a get away with bullshit—get away with murder free card for as long as I could remember.

Lena closes her eyes a moment, those dark half-moons pressed with charcoal shadow fold in on themselves like Russian nesting dolls. Lena's eyelids have been getting progressively fragile and crepey. We inherited our thin skin from our mother, among other far more indistinguishable features such as our inability to tell the truth. As much as I appreciate starting over in Percy Bay, it feels as if we're building a sandcastle. I can feel the tide shifting, see the waves coming. It won't be pretty when it hits. It never is.

"It wasn't her." Lena gives a hard sigh. "Don't do this to yourself. She's not out to get us anymore." She shoots a cold glance out the window as if she were having a hard time buying this bullshit herself. Her gaze narrows over my shoulder. "The Chandelier is hosting a fundraiser for the community center next weekend out on the pier. Bring

Bram and the kids. I know for a fact they'll be there." She casts a quick glance their way once again as they light up the room with cackles. My sister's eyes meet up with mine. "Please."

"A fundraiser? I mingled with a corpse at that last one. No thank you."

"You'll need this if you want to fit in, believe me. There's no escaping these social circles. The best thing to do is make amends. Play nice then fade into the background like a good little girl. Your reward will be raising your kids in a stable environment. You can't live on the run your whole lives, Ree."

"I know." I steal a quick glance over my shoulder as Astrid leans in hard across the table. Her white skintight jeans show off the perfect heart of her bottom, and I can't help but scowl at her. I hate the thought of having her around Bram. Stupid, I know, but it doesn't change the fact I feel that way. Bridget catches my eye, and her lip curls into a half-smile. It spells out danger more than it does anything amicable, so I turn back around. "I'll do it."

"You will?" Lena lifts a carefully lined brow. Lena has always exercised her right to emulate a Disney villain.

"Yes. But only because you have to be there and endure their wrath. I'll be your buffer."

She gives me a swift kick under the table. "I'm your buffer, and you know it."

"I know it." I kiss the lip of my mug and take a careful sip. I glance back at the cocky hens to my right, and Astrid turns to look my way, her eyes slit to nothing. There's an inherent coldness about her, and I've felt this from the beginning. I've got news for Lena—these ladies don't know the meaning of the word *nice*.

Lena shakes her head, and those dark bangs cut rigid and uneven flirt with her brows. "Your paranoia is on high. It's not Mom."

I give a slight nod as if agreeing, but, deep down, I'm afraid it is.

Someone is watching me. Perhaps having me watched. Yes, my paranoia is on high. Someone has died. Someone is calling out to me, calling me out. Regardless, something is happening. And I have a foreboding feeling this will not end well.

Four

Bram

Hennessy is a bustling town three and a half hours north of Percy Bay, so I've pitched for a hotel room. Correction— Smile Wide has pitched for a hotel room, a nice one with a balcony facing a river to my left, the trash receptacles behind the hotel to my right.

There is a full bar and a shower roomy enough to fit my entire family, and how I wish they were here with me to fill it. Not that I've made it a practice to shower with them all in number. Lena's old swimming pool was as close as we ever got to that endeavor. But being here without them, anywhere without them, makes them feel less real, a dream that is slowly evaporating.

A very real part of me is frightened that I will wake up and it will be the day after Simone's body was discovered—the body I discovered. That my beautiful wife, present tense, my beautiful children, were just a work of my overactive imagination. It's terrifying to think about. My old life, the one I shared for years with Simone, was tense, cloying, filled with terrors far before our kids ever set foot into the lake that fateful day. Simone had the skills to suck the air out of the room and leave you choking for your next breath. She may have been witty and intelligent—she certainly could do anything better than me as she used to sing. She was as sharp as a blade in every arena, but she was a loaded gun that was pointed at my temple, at my beating heart every minute we shared together.

The dental convention is held in a cavernous hall somewhere buried beneath this labyrinth-like structure. Tarquin, one of my colleagues who happens to own the practice, gifted me the honor to attend today's riveting panels. As the low man on the totem pole, it was apparent it would be me going from the start. One might think in a large practice of nine dentists there would be an outcry over who had the chance to enjoy a free night in a hotel with the peace and quiet of the river—the dental convention itself is somewhat interesting if not strictly informative, but, in truth, dentists by and large are content residing in their own habitat. Fingers flexing in and out of other people's mouths. It's not nearly as sexual in nature as it sounds. It's quite mundane, but I will admit, it is personal, intimate in some respects.

That's why when our neighbor, chicken lover extraordinaire, Astrid Nelson, strutted into the office yesterday and landed in my chair—*my chair*—I marveled at the coincidence, but when she gave that sly bedroom-eye look, I quickly realized it was most likely no coincidence. Perhaps the secretary's palm was greased a little money, perhaps it was a twisted version of fate, but something did not feel right. And as soon as I started probing around at that problem area she claimed to have, her tongue caressed my gloved finger in a manner that let me know she was up for my probing fingers to land elsewhere.

I try my best to brush Astrid and her wet mouth out of my mind as I take the elevator down. I've missed the initial sign-in, the keynote, and most likely the first session. The traffic over was thicker than expected. Soccer moms seemed to fill the highways and every side street at ungodly hours, bussing their sleepy children to better schools far out of range.

The elevator spits me out on the lobby level and I step out, the convention an entire floor beneath me, and I cringe as the doors whoosh shut from behind. I press the button and wait impatiently with my hand clutching my briefcase, a caramel leather box my mother bought for me last Christmas. My mother was a gossip columnist in New York, a successful one at that, but her time has come and gone. The era of paparazzi had eaten her career in a single bound, and now she is relegated to the odd interview on what it's like to have gone from a who's who to a has-been. I give the button a few more spastic twitches, looking like the quintessential businessman, an important one at that, who has far too many places to be at once. I like the narrative far better than the real one, the dental practitioner who lost his family, his practice, and his mind all in one year's time. The low man on the totem pole who is stuck on the wrong floor at the wrong hour wondering if he is going to spend the rest of his life in this strange limbo, anticipating someone to point the finger at me and say those words I dread to hear: it's you.

The click of heels struts by, and like some testosterone-fueled ape, my head turns lazily in their direction. My eyes hook on a somewhat familiar frame, petite, wavy dark hair that seems to bounce in rhythm with the girl's footsteps, and I do a neck breaking double take. My entire body does a one-eighty, and I hear the elevator doors open and close behind me.

My eyes latch over her person with a macabre sense of wonder, of outright fear. My feet move swiftly toward her. The businessman with too many directions to move in has chosen the wrong one. I step in line with her, ten paces behind, six, then three. I'm close enough to touch her, and as soon as we hit the end of the foyer, I snatch her by the elbow and spin her around. My hands fall over her shoulders, caging her in.

"Holy shit," I mutter as I take her in, same dark eyes, those easy lips that have wrapped themselves around every part of my body.

Her lips part, a strange croaking sound dislodges as if she wasn't sure who I was, and she steps backwards cautiously at first, her face, still pretty, hardened with time, knife sharp lines embedded around her mouth, evidence she still smokes.

She gives a subtle shake of the head before darting in

the opposite direction, her strides evening out as she darts down a carpeted corridor, and just like that, it's over.

Loretta. I lean against the wall as if I needed it to hold me upright. I'm so very relieved not a word was exchanged, and why would it be? She doesn't want to know me. Nobody in their right mind does. I close my eyes a moment, and those countless hotel rooms zoom by like a slide show. My eyes spring wide again, and my feet start working as I head to the nearest elevator, ambling my way to the hornets' nest of dental pride on this side of the coast. A couple of girls, no older than teenagers, sign me in and give me my badge to wear with pride, Bram Woodley Liar at Large, and my hand shakes as I take it.

Someway, somehow, my present collided with my past this afternoon. Those blood red pots that took up residence on the stove this morning ring through my mind like a bell. I don't absorb a thing about thrilling new dental products as I wander aimlessly up and down the cluttered aisles with their euphoric sales teams and shiny new gadgets. I pay little attention at the seminar regarding insurance. There is no volition in me to try out the new dental products when I'm asked to participate. No. I'm only here in body, not in any other capacity. At noon, I sit alone facing a stone wall on the outdoor patio while pretending to eat a generous portion of prime rib. I can't take a bite.

And once the final breakout session of the day is over, a refresher course on computer solutions, I head straight for my room, lock the door, and meander to the window to catch a glimpse of the river, something calming, and God knows I could use a tranquilizer right about now. But I don't look left to the river. Instead, my gaze shifts right. It has to. It's practically demanded of it. The asphalt around the dumpsters is inundated with men in navy jackets, and miles of bright yellow caution tape cuts through the monochromatic day like an obstruction, sunny lasers that eat up your eyes. A white blanket lies over a body in the center of the melee, and I can't breathe. There is no air left in this room. My body slaps numb with shock, and a bite of sweat ignites under my arms. One dark clump of wavy hair peers out from the tarp they've set over her, and my stomach churns hot.

Holy shit. It's happening. A strange feeling comes over me. I've stepped onto a haunted carousel, and there's no way to safely get off.

My body bucks and I stagger for the bathroom, but vomit hard into the wastebasket instead. I run my face under the faucet for a small eternity before coming to and throwing my things back into my suitcase. I don't spend the night. I head home to my family, drive three and a half hours listening to the news. Homicide behind the Hennessy Continental Hotel. An unidentified young woman found strangled, her hand maimed.

I slam my palm over the steering wheel as I eat asphalt trying to make my way to Percy, to Ree, to my children whom I'm terrified will never know me past their youth. Everything is unraveling. Everything is coming undone.

Everything I've feared has come to pass.

Loretta is dead. Is she? How I wish it were anyone else. But this is me, my luck I've tainted her with. Just one touch and she's gone.

Something horrible has happened.

It's still happening.

Five

Ree

May 21st

Peter had another seminar in Manhattan yesterday, and in a fit of nostalgia—and longing to have a sexy escape with my husband, I joined him. I arranged for Kelly to show just after nine. Peter drove out at six thirty. I didn't tell him I would be inviting myself as his plus one, but then, I didn't think I had to. I thought what fun! How totally awesome to surprise a man who can never be surprised! I could hardly wait to see him. I treated myself to coffee and lunch in midtown, bought a new pair of shoes in an upscale boutique—a treat I felt I had earned after a long week with the twins. Who are we kidding? A long eight years! I jest! Not really, but that derails my point. I had earned them, and they were delicious, calling out to me in that cantaloupe color I crave on occasion. So I put them on, drove to Javits Center, and made my way to the convention floor where I knew I would find my husband, but he never showed. I asked the girls in charge to please let me know if he made it to the meeting, and they looked at me as if I were a certifiable stalker. So I did the only thing I could think to do without ruining the surprise. I scouted his services location. He was miles away, close to the pricey cantaloupe shoe shop (which burned me. Do you know how futile driving in the city is? It feels like a slow death). But I found him. At Renata's restaurant—coming out of Renata's just as I ran up the block. (Have I mentioned parking is impossible?) I found him.

I don't know how to say this. I don't want to. For some reason, putting it down in black and white makes it feel so real, so final. I saw Peter walking along the street with his arm around the shoulders of a tiny brunette. My God, at first glance, I thought she was a child! A prepubescent teenager in the least. She was young. Younger than me. Pretty from afar. You know the type, va va voom figure, curvy but not stalky. Hair for miles. I froze in the street like a stop sign. My heart thumped wildly in my ears, eating away the sound of the traffic. The people bustling around me melted away like snow. At first, I thought this is simply a colleague. Someone from dental school perhaps? But then, his hand slipped down to the small of her back. So very intimate, and I knew.

All of my dark suspicions had been realized in that moment. I have never felt good enough for Peter. Not pretty enough, certainly not smart enough, not enough as a whole.

What had gone wrong? If I was lacking in bed, one would think he would have the decency to let me in on it and then teach me what he wanted. How had this become our life? I followed them a half a block before they ducked into the Grand Regency, and I couldn't breathe. My feet stalled again like a car with a bad engine. A part of me wanted to run in screaming. A part of me was over it, done with Peter altogether. But the very reason I came to Manhattan to begin with was nestled deep inside of me. I was going to surprise Peter with our big news. And it was me who was left speechless.

Surprise!

"Ree?" Bram calls from the hall, and I'm quick to close the book and bury it in its tomb beneath a pile of sweaters. I step into my heels, trot out to the mirror, and inspect my black cocktail dress, my simple string of pearls.

He steps in, his cologne permeating the space between us before he ever arrives, and then there he is, a sports coat, dark inky jeans, those gorgeous low-cut boots I bought him for Christmas. His hair is still glossed from the shower, slicked back, his face peppered with dark stubble the way I love it, and it makes his eyes glow ten times brighter. Bram is a vision, and yet my heart sinks at the sight of him.

"I'm ready." I snap my clutch off the dresser, and we head out the door together.

———— • • • ————

The fundraiser that the Blue Chandelier is putting on is being held on the waterfront. The boardwalk has been transformed with miles of tables that hold items for a silent auction, and the people of Percy Bay have come out in number to help with the cause. It's a family event, so there are plenty of kids here, all neatly compartmentalized in a large grassy field with a bounce house and games they can play for free. Mila, Tessa's oldest daughter, a junior in high school, offers to keep an eye on them for me while Bram and I head for the auction site.

I spot Lena in her chef's garb, her face intent as she listens to a few women from the PTA while passing out canapés from the tray she's holding.

"Can you believe this is the new us?" Bram lands a warm kiss just under my ear and, instinctually, I turn my head without meaning to.

"Yes," it comes out less than a whisper as I take in the briny air. A cool breeze is blowing steadily, and I'm thankful I decided to put my hair up for the evening. Everywhere you look women are struggling to shake their tresses out of their eyes. But my heart and my head are far away from the boardwalk. I look to Bram and force a tight smile, taking up his hand as we head into the thick of Percy's precarious social circles.

A part of me screams, *tell him about the shitty emails, tell him about the diary, for God's sake*. It's only going to get worse as time passes, and yet another part of me is all too aware that Bram never mentioned he and Simone were trying for another baby. He never mentioned that he was anything but faithful to her.

"I was thinking—" I bite down on my lip, and Bram whisks us behind a tent that's housing handmade crafts as it swarms with women.

His arms wrap around my waist, and an easy smile glides over his lips.

"What's wrong?" His brows dip a moment. "I know you like I know myself. Something has thrown you. Let me in, Ree." He dots a kiss over my lips. "I want to see the world through your eyes."

My stomach melts right down to my feet, and I soften in his warm embrace, my lips twitching toward the sky. This is Bram. Peter is gone. Peter and Simone are gone. They are no more. And yet a part of me can't seem to forgive him for a slight that was never toward me. A horrible thought slaps through me, and my body stiffens once again. Bram was out of town—at a convention just a few days ago. Certainly an opportunity. What if this brunette is still hanging around on the periphery of his life? For a moment, I picture the two of them laughing at me while she obliges him with blowjobs. The entire idea is ridiculous, and yet it has me fuming.

I suck in my bottom lip, trying to look seductive while

hiding the fear rising in me. I had never thought Simone and I had a thing in common outside our shared husband— not that Bram and I are legally wed, but that's another horror I don't want to digest at the moment. But after reading her journals, really getting to know her on an intimate level, we not only share similar careers—okay, her career, my hobby, but we share the same insecurities.

"Did you ever think about having more children?" My God, is that the best I could do?

Bram tips his head back, and a quick laugh bounces through him. "Is that what this is all about?" He swoops in with another kiss, his features growing serious—so morbidly handsome it frightens me. "Aubree," he whispers my name like a secret. "Yes. If that's what you want, that's what we'll do."

"We can't afford it," I say, stunned that he went straight for the gold. Certainly not the turn I was expecting, but then, I walked him right into it.

"We will be fine." He shakes his head sweetly before brushing a loose wisp of hair that's lying over my forehead. "And we can start tonight." There's an ache in his voice, a tenderness I can't deny. Bram is intent on making me feel better, pulling me out of the funk I'm in. The funk he thinks my urge to have a child put me in, and ironically it was his ex-wife who landed me neck deep. "Baby making." He gives a dark gurgle of a laugh, and those comma-like dimples go off that I love so much.

"Baby making," I parrot back, playing along. In truth, I'm not sure I'm up for a third just yet, but I love the fact that Bram is so keen on the idea that I might just let him sway me with his enthusiasm.

We head back out to the crowd, and a group of men shout for him over by the wine tasting booth.

"Ah! Work never ends." He winks my way. Bram leads us over and introduces me to his colleagues. I've met two before but not the entire herd. They're all affable looking men, around the same age as Bram, some a bit older. Tarquin is technically his boss, the owner of Smile Wide. He wears a halo of gray and holds a rounded belly compared to the much more fit group that surrounds him. Bram is the most handsome of them all, but then, I am bias. After a brief introduction, the shorter one, Rich, with a head of hair that's been reduced to stubbles, tips his beer Bram's way.

"Tell us about Hennessy. Geez. Was that nuts? Did you hear or see anything suspicious?"

Bram shoots a quick glance my way, his eyes oscillate a moment as if he weren't sure what direction to look in next as he takes a deep breath, and suddenly, my attention is aroused.

"What happened?" I give his hand a quick tug.

Bram winces my way, something about that half-wink, that grimace sets my teeth on edge.

Tarquin cuts his hand through the air. "He's talking about the body. Sorry. It's not pleasant conversation." He nods to Rich as if to say *knock it off*. The conversation quickly morphs into shoptalk, and I spot Lena out by the edge of the pier and excuse myself.

Body? My God, why wouldn't Bram have mentioned a *body*? I mean, that's pretty serious, right? A twinge of guilt coats me. It's not as if I've been forthcoming with everything lately myself. And in his defense, he probably didn't want to upset me.

I bump into Lena and steal a cracker loaded with something creamy from off her tray and indulge angrily as I swallow it down all but whole. I can't help but feel as if I'm drowning, and I inwardly cringe at the analogy. Those are words I've been careful never to utter to Bram. It hasn't been easy. It's a euphemism I used to spill as easy as water. There I go again. Only this time I'm a little angry with him, so I don't mind doing it.

"Someone's in a hostile mood." Lena tweaks her brows as if she were about to pull me under another ten feet—no air for me tonight. "What's going on?" She nods, pointing behind me with her nose. "Those witches getting under your skin again?"

I turn to find the trio of terror—not that Tessa is much of a terror. She actually bought me coffee after Peanut Butter Gate, and that was rather kind of her, considering she was brave enough to cavort with a food criminal.

Bridget looks dressed to slash and thrash in a tight red dress, her long wavy hair bouncing as if it weren't even connected to her scalp. And I can't help but notice that Astrid looks sleek in a black and white pantsuit that seems to elongate her legs for miles. She's donned a halter-top, brave, considering the fog is rolling in. But her bare shoulders, that deep red lipstick she's paired it with, makes her look as if she just stepped off a runway. She turns slightly, and then we see it. Both Lena and I groan in unison.

"My God, she is certifiable." My sister chokes on a laugh.

"You took the words right out of my mouth." Only I would have been a touch cruder.

Cradled in Astrid's arms is that glossy feathered cock of hers, pecking at her chest as if it were thirsty for something she had to offer.

Lena clicks her tongue. "Ten bucks says she lets the thing suck on her tits when no one is looking."

"Lena!" I swat her and share a dark laugh with my sister. Just past them Astrid's husband, Miles, stands with Bridget's husband, Jude, and the two of them look as if they're immersed in a heavy conversation. Every now and again, they turn to look solemnly at their wives. Most likely contemplating how they managed to steal their balls. Speaking of husbands with no balls. "You know that convention Bram went to last week? Apparently, there was a body," I say without the slightest knowledge of any other detail.

"Yes." Her pale eyes pin to mine. "And did you hear how they found the body?"

A rush of adrenaline hits me for no reason, an uncalled for pinprick of panic that dislodges my senses for a moment. "No. How?"

"A wire wrapped around her neck reducing it to the size of a thimble."

I suck in a sharp breath, and I see her again, lying there on the floor of the school gymnasium.

Lena nods. "A finger missing."

"Oh my God."

"Oh my yes," Lena muses. "There's a serial killer running loose amongst us." She offers a slow, circular nod. "Wait. You said Bram was at that convention? Was he at the Hennessy Convention Center?"

My body lurches in one large detonating heartbeat. "Yes, I guess he was."

"Shit." Her eyes close, and I'd swear on all that is holy the daylight around me just dimmed a notch. Lena's eyes have always held their own brand of wattage. "You guys have the shittiest luck of anyone I know."

My own eyes close for a moment as my fingers clasp

over my mouth. "God help us. Let's just pray the authorities don't connect the mismatched dots. It's just a coincidence, that's all."

"Is it really?" She takes a disbelieving step away. "I guess it boils down to how well do you know and trust your husband."

"Now you're just being ridiculous. You know Bram wouldn't hurt a fly." I glance in his direction, and there's a huge migration of bodies blooming between us, kids with cotton candy swirled to the sky, women strutting about, happy to have traded their winter boots for wedges. Men with their leering gazes, eyes shifting toward hemlines, flitting to the nearest décolletage. The sea of pedestrians parts and there he is, and my stomach sinks like a milestone. Gone are his cohorts in dental crime. In their place stands a hell of a cocky woman and her pet fowl writhing between them. Bram laughs openly at something she says, and that knot in my stomach tightens. Her hand rides up his arm, and I inch back at the surprise of seeing her touch him so brazenly. Bram doesn't resist. Instead, he leans in and speaks directly to her, intently, and my mind demands I go over there and toss Astrid into the water behind her. A bath in harbor sludge should rectify the behavior.

"Relax," Lena says it low, far too controlled as if she were trying to hold me back emotionally, but we both know she's failing. "It's just a conversation."

"Says the girl who had me doubting him less than ten seconds ago."

A salted breeze whistles by, and I take in the briny air, trying to bring myself back down to earth.

Bram takes a step in. He's shaking his head, saying something with those serious eyes, that thoughtful tilt of the head. Then his lids lower just a notch, and I'm sick. He's bedroom-eyeing her. My God, it can't be. This is Bram. My Bram. I'm hallucinating the entire event. Astrid's dolt of a husband joins the party, and the two of them break apart like a couple of naughty teenagers caught making out in the closet. Sickening. My entire body bucks in disbelief.

Lena steps in and effectively blocks my view with her body. "Have you had any more of those strange emails?" She shakes her head as if the answer should be no. I've already told her about the two.

99

"No. Thank God."

"Who do you think is sending them?"

"My guess is the cocky one who thinks it's fine to flirt with my husband out in the open."

"That may be so, but I just so happened to receive my own unexpected email from someone this afternoon, and I thought you should read it." Her eyes linger over mine for a moment too long before she fishes her phone out of her pocket and pulls the email up for me to see.

My eyes gloss over the words in a hurry, trying to discern the danger my sister might be in, and my heart ceases beating altogether. A breath hitches in my throat.

"No," it's all I can manage. My blood pressure spikes to unsafe levels. Adrenaline shoots through my veins in one violent burst. "This can't be happening. This will not happen."

Lena pulls the phone to her chest before I can snatch it from her and toss it into the water. Her eyes set to mine with a fire in them that I have never seen.

"It is and it will."

Six

Bram

All the way home Ree is angry. I wait until we shuffle the kids to their rooms to get ready for bed before I corner my wife in our bedroom.

Ree flicks off her shoes wildly, and I'm alarmed on every level. For as long as I've known my sweet wife, she has been just that, sweet. And, believe me, it held great appeal to me, especially after the war I had fought with Simone. Ree was the proverbial drink of water that this thirsty man had longed for in so many ways.

She darts for the closet, and I grab her by the elbow, spinning her into me as if we were doing some exotic heated dance. Her elbows butt up against my chest, holding a firm distance between us.

"What's going on?" I temper my voice, pull it down a few notches, soft and soothing, hoping she'll come along for the ride. I've never been one to read women well. My understanding of the opposite sex has always been limited to the here and now, the black and the white. I am colorblind when we drift into the gray zone, and if I've learned anything in this life, it's that women mostly live in the gray zone. "Did someone say something to upset you? Was it those women again?"

She lets out a vitriolic huff as if I should know better, as if to say how dare I suggest it, and I can feel my neck growing hot because I can't stand the suspense. Ree doesn't get mad. So if she's pissed, this must be big.

"It was my sister." She yanks free from my hold and takes a full step back. "My mother contacted her. She'll be in town next weekend."

"Your mother?" I mouth the words. I have never dared bring her up first. The only conversations we've had about that certifiable nutcase have been initiated by Ree herself, and I can count those on one hand and have a healthy amount of fingers left over.

"Yes. The beast who bore me. And get this." She hikes an arm in the air, flailing to the ceiling, and I catch the glint of tears in her eyes. "She's staying with Lena! *Fucking* Lena!" Her voice screeches to new heights, and I wrap my arm around her again and whisk us into the bathroom to dampen her fury from the children's prying ears.

"Shit," it's all I can say. The only thing that comes to mind when I think of that woman and what she's done to Ree—to Lena, too, and that's what makes this entire scenario somewhat unbelievable.

"Yes, shit," she barks it out with rage. Ree averts her eyes a moment before deflating. "It turns out, Lena has been in communication with her for the last few months. Nothing serious. Just a tap here. A *how do you do* there. And all this time, I thought Lena was on my side—*our* side. Hell, I didn't know I was on a damned island." Her voice grows threadbare as if she were about to cry.

"Come here." I pull her in, and her body bucks against mine a moment. "It's going to be all right." Except it isn't, considering the fact Lena has set up camp across the street. Damned hippie. If she really cared about Ree—about herself, she would never have let it get this far.

"It's not going to be all right, Bram. You don't know my mother. You have no idea the evil that woman is capable of." Her watery eyes look to mine, a clear ocean of amber. Twin pools unwilling to give up their tears. Ree has always held a princess appeal, and tonight she looks like exactly that.

Lilly howls for us, and we take a simultaneous breath.

"Let's get the kids to bed." I tuck a kiss under her jawline. "And then we can get to the task of making a new kid." I give a playful shrug. "Or practice. I think we're getting a little rusty."

Her cheeks brighten a warm shade of red. Ree has always managed to look smitten to be with me, grateful to be with me, and it feels awkward to admit that. Ree is gorgeous in her own right, and all that monster who's about to barrel into town has ever done has made Ree think otherwise.

"I love you," I whisper. "And if I didn't say it earlier, you looked stunning tonight."

"You can cool it with the come-ons." She gives the lip of my jeans a quick tug. "You're getting laid, Dr. Woodley."

I flinch internally when she says my proper moniker. We haven't spoken it out loud since our last move. And strangely, it feels as if she's just unleashed a curse into the room, slithering between us like a snake.

We share a dark, delicious kiss before putting the kids to bed.

Ree and I hit the sheets and set them on fire, set each other on fire. Yes, another child would be nice, would be a blessing. But I can't help feeling a little bit cursed these days—hell, I've never felt otherwise.

All night I toss and turn. Somewhere between four and five in the morning Ree gets up, no lights, tiptoes to the restroom, but she doesn't come back to bed. Instead, she heads into her closet and closes the door, leaving a seam of light slicing through the murky darkness. She doesn't come out for a good long while, and it makes me wonder.

• ◆ •

On Monday, somewhere between setting a crown and a routine dental exam, my phone buzzes in my pocket. I'm not one to pick up when I'm with a patient, but I'm mid-stream, walking between one room and the next. Here at Smile Wide, the philosophy is juggle two clients at once. The billing is phenomenal, only I wouldn't know it because I happened to sign on as salary.

I glare down at my phone a moment. It's a number I don't recognize, so I let it go to voicemail, but something in me says wait it out. Sure enough, there's a message.

"Hello, this is Detective Rivera from the Hennessy Police Department calling about a recent homicide you might have information about. Please call me back at your earliest convenience. I'd love to ask you a few questions."

Ice courses through my veins. My feet have screwed themselves into the floor. Can't move. The convention. Loretta. Shit. Shit. Shit.

It takes all my willpower to get through the rest of the day before I meet my brother for drinks down at the Thirsty Fox, a dive bar on the edge of town that splits the distance between our homes.

The Thirsty Fox is on the last decent street before you segue into a homeless encampment. It's dark inside, save for the dim lighting emitting from a yellow neon sign that sits behind the bar itself like a homing beacon for all the drunks that infiltrate this place. It holds the scent of hard liquor and peanuts, and somehow the lively atmosphere makes up for the fact it's located in the ass-crack of town.

No sign of Mace, so I belly up to the bar, take a seat on the end, and a beer magically appears before me.

It was a bar just like this one that I met Ree in. I still think of that dark rainy night. What a miraculous coincidence it was that we were there together—two lost souls intersecting at just the right time in one another's lives. How horrific it would have been if either of us didn't show up. But a part of me holds a romantic ideal that we would have met anyway, at a bus stop, simply walking down the street, in line for a movie. That the universe had no choice but to arrange for it. I'm not a big believer in destinies, especially not after the shit parade my life with Simone had become. But with Ree, I could practically hear destiny calling. When I least expected it, I looked up, and there she was.

I turn my head to the left as a wistful nod to fate and shudder when I see an all too familiar blonde.

"Astrid?"

Her pale face breaks into a giant mischievous grin, and I can feel the acid percolating in my stomach.

"Well, hello, sexy." She shakes her chest half-heartedly as she plops in the seat next to me. She lifts a finger at the bartender. "Long Island Iced Tea." Those glowing eyes revert back to mine. "What brings you down to this shithole? Drinking your troubles away so soon after moving to Percy?" Her shoulder brushes against mine, and my stomach sours. Astrid has been to my office on three different occasions now, all bullshit excuses to arrange for my fingers to probe around in her mouth.

The secretary confirmed she requests me personally. She even offered up a mocking laugh when she implied Astrid had something akin to a schoolgirl crush. But here we are in a bar, together. And God knows something like this can be misconstrued to mean something different. Small towns are known to talk, and I'm not in the mood for something different. I may have behaved one way with Simone, but with her I was both worn down and stupid at the same time. A toxic combination if ever there was one. But with Ree, I am straight as an arrow, not because I feel compelled by fear, but because I love my wife. She is the only woman I want to be with for the rest of my life. The only woman my heart can see. And how I wish my eyes weren't seeing the one before me. Ree is it for me. My love story ends with her.

And the dark and bleak truth is that I wish Ree were my wife from the beginning, not Simone, never Simone. I wish that Isla and Henry were ours right along with Lilly and Jack. A horrible part of me wishes I could blip Simone out of the radar of my life as far back as that day we met. Another part of me is convinced that Isla and Henry would be here if Ree were in charge. I'm not sure why I never placed the blame on the sitter. Logic would deem so, but Simone was at the water that day with them, absorbed in her damned laptop. Ree would have saved it for later and had fun with the kids. She knows how fleeting childhood can be. She just so happened to have missed her own.

"I'm meeting up with a friend." I'm not sure why I went with the lie. But something tells me once she finds out I have a brother, it will put Mace squarely on her very married radar.

Her tongue rims her lips as she rocks her body, bumping into me every other second. "What kind of friend?" Her shoe runs along my leg, a cheesy move if ever there was one.

"Just an old buddy. It's nothing more than a friendly hello." I pull my beer forward. "Just like this."

Her affect falters, from lust to anger, zero to sixty. "Hon, you and I both know I'd like to be much more than friends." Her teeth graze her bottom lip. Her skin is sagging around her eyes, her makeup encrusted along the edges. "Consider it an open invite anytime you're up for trying something new."

I swallow hard, uncertain what to do with this sober invite. It's frightening and makes me wonder how this will be used against me. In my world, that's how this kind of a thing works. Every disaster, real and imagined, has always fallen squarely over my shoulders.

A warm laugh rattles in my chest. "I'm quite all right. Your husband seems nice. Good man." I point over at her as I suck down as much of my beer as I can. The quicker I can dilute reality, the better.

"He's all right. If you're up for that kind of thing." Her finger traces over my thigh in the shape of an S and I snatch up her hand before she hits pay dirt. She glowers at me a moment before taking her wrist back. "An eviction notice has been circling my brain as far as he's concerned. I'm not there anymore. Not present in the marriage. There's just something missing. The man hardly makes me feel alive." Her eyes widen as she leans in far too close. "It takes a special man to make me feel alive, Bram. A gorgeous man like yourself with fire in his eyes, a zest for life. You make me feel emotions that I never thought possible. In fact, you have managed to garner the attention of every woman in Percy the second you showed up in town. How is that, Bram? What kind of a spell did you cast on the women of this town to make that happen?" Her fingers dig into the back of my hair, and I back up just enough until she surrenders her position.

"Fine." She holds her palm out at me. "Have it your way, but know this. I've seen that wifey of yours, met her, spoke with her in depth. She won't keep you settled for long. A man like you needs someone vivacious, someone who's up for anything, and I'm guessing she's not." She gulps down her drink in record time and slams the glass onto the table. "Enjoy your missionary position life. And enjoy that beer. I suddenly realize why you need it so badly." She takes off, and her perfume lingers in the vacuum of her wake. I can feel it fashioning a rose-scented noose and circling my neck. Astrid is trouble. If I'm not careful, she will most certainly and enthusiastically come back to bite me in the ass.

Mason shows up as if on cue and slaps me over the back as he takes her seat.

"Making friends?" he teases.

"You and I both know I'm only capable of making enemies." And there are no truer words than that.

"You look like shit." He sheds a quick grin. Mace and I have always been cautious regarding our happiness. After our father took off for greener marital pastures, it seemed he took the familial horseshoe with him. Neither Mace nor I have ever been able to catch a break. He's up a divorce on me, but I'm up one dead wife.

"I was about to say the same about you. Thanks for coming out."

Mace nods to the bartender, and two fresh beers land before us. I suck the foam off of mine before indulging in a few hearty gulps.

"Homicide detective down in Hennessy wants to speak with me."

The whites of his eyes shoot my way. My brother has always been my older lookalike, save for his salt and pepper hair. The salt is winning. He blames me, of course, all that worrying about his baby brother. I always said my hair never bothered to turn because I was too damn afraid to worry.

I blow out a slow breath. "It's about Loretta."

His brows bounce. "She's dead." He offers an odd congratulatory nod as if everyone associated with me were somehow required to die. Some demonic feat that needed to be met. "But I already knew that." His expression sours again. "In fact, I'm one step ahead of you." He pulls up a picture on his phone and shoves it my way.

"Oh God," it's all I can muster. There I am in black and white, my hands on her shoulders, her face filled with fear. Her beautiful face.

"Yes, oh God," he parrots without the right emotion behind it. "You are fucked, my friend. What the hell were you thinking?"

"How did you get that?" I take a moment to marvel at my brother's stealth detective skills. In all honesty, when he set out to be a caped-crusader, I didn't have all that much faith in him. Low self-worth has always been the great Woodley curse, and I never thought to contest it.

"Never mind how I got it. Did you kill this woman?"

he hisses it out low enough, but the hair on the back of my neck curls nonetheless. This woman. I met *that* woman in a bar much like this one, but in Manhattan during one of the many city runs I made to escape a marriage that was wearing me down. I thought she was a friendly girl, pretty, and one thing led to a hotel room. Turns out, she liked to meet men in bars for fun and for a little cash on the side. She never charged me, which, of course, fed my ridiculous ego.

"No. I did not." I lean in, pissed as hell. "Do not breathe those words to me ever again. I was at—"

"A dental convention," he muses. "Do you know her little finger was removed with a surgical instrument? One, say, that a *dentist* might have access to?"

I shake my head at the implication.

Mace leans in, those dark caterpillar brows of his do a little dance along his forehead. "Do you remember who else had a finger missing?"

"Shit." It's as if someone unplugged the entire world, and the room grows strangely dim. The music grinds down to destitute levels. It's all I can do to remain upright.

"Hey"—Mace grips me by the arm and gives a hearty

shake—"do not pass out on me. Pull it together."

I drag my eyes to meet with my brother's. Growing up, it was always Mace who came to my rescue. It was Mace who warded off the bullies and the bad guys. After our father took off, it was Mace who was the man of the house, thereby allowing me to be the carefree kid who would eventually make enough mistakes for the both of us—for the neighborhood, hell, for the entire Western Hemisphere.

"Who's doing this?" The words crawl out of my throat like maggots. "And why?"

"Pete, if I knew that, I wouldn't be sitting here. I'd be tracking down the motherfucker with a machete." The muscles in his jaw pop because he meant every word. "But I do believe somewhere in that ball of knowledge that sits on your shoulders lies the answers. Who did you infuriate?" He shakes his head, his demanding stone blue eyes heavily glued to mine.

I gulp down half my beer trying to solve the riddle of the Sphinx. "Erwin Wilson is serving a life sentence under psychiatric care for the murder of my wife." I glance to Mace, and he shakes his head.

"Try again."

A moment of strained silence thickens the air between us. The moment I stop believing that Erwin Wilson bludgeoned Simone in our living room all those frightening years ago is the moment I begin to unravel.

"That's the real reason I called you here." I rap my knuckles against the bar as if calling court to order, a foreboding irony in and of itself. "I think we need to peel back the past, one painful layer at a time." I hold him firmly in my gaze while my heart does the death rattle on its way up my throat. Once I say the next few words, all hell is going to break loose. Who am I kidding? It already has. "Deep down, I have always questioned Erwin's involvement with Simone's murder."

His eyes widen just a touch. "Forensics—"

"I don't give a shit about forensics." I lean in hard, glaring at this older version of myself without meaning to. "I do not care about the judicial system that put him behind bars either. Something nefarious has been eating up my existence and those around me ever since I lost Isla and Henry." My vocal cords threaten to knot up when I say their names. My God, I don't think I've so much as whispered them ever since that night I shared their names with Ree. I haven't even spoken of them to Lilly and Jack. Ree has been the translator of all things macabre. She's been the rock I've needed her to be, my mouthpiece, the binding which holds my sanity together.

Mace takes a deep breath, widening his chest to the size of a city. "You want me to reopen my investigation?"

I give a single nod. I know what a shit ride it was the first time. The endless hours that were lost all dragging us in one slow, bloody circle. We ended at the same place we started, with nothing. The police arrested Erwin relatively quickly, less than twenty-four hours into their investigation. It all seemed like such a relief at the time, but in the back of my mind, it felt a little too easy, a little too convenient for my complicated life. I was still guilty in the court of public opinion.

Erwin was prosecuted quickly and shuffled off to what amounts to a detention center for the criminally insane, and that was it. One big neat judicial bow was put on the case, and I was free to go on with the rest of my life. But that nagging feeling that this was wrong, that this, whatever *this* is, was far from over, never quite left me.

Not before Ree, not after.

I have never been able to shake the feeling that lurking in the shadows of my life was someone, something waiting to burn everything down around me. My dead children, my dead wife were not enough. I could feel its thirst for me ramping up. And yet I wondered what more there was to give. But now there are three things, three people I would go to the ends of the earth to protect, and I will.

"This is where you come in," I whisper as I knock my beer softly to his. "You, my brother, are going to figure out this jigsaw puzzle that something far more evil than fate has thrown at my feet. I don't think it was a coincidence anymore that Ree found that body at the school function a few weeks back. I don't think it was a coincidence that Loretta St. James ended up dead at the same hotel I was staying at. And I don't want to wait until another seeming coincidence pops up in my life."

A thought hits me, a brick wall of a revelation that I had openly overlooked up until now.

"Her finger was missing." I blink over at my brother, stifling the urge to vomit. "The woman Ree found. The prostitute."

Mace looks dazed as if I had thrown him. It's not uncommon for us to berate my shitty life when we get together, but today I took it up to a whole other level. Not to mention the fact I'm dragging him right back into my personal wormhole.

"Where do I start?" He gives his beer an absentminded twirl. "I'll see about getting in and speaking with Erwin again."

"Good." Something in me loosens as if our feet had finally hit terra firma again after all these years. "I'm going with you."

"I didn't think you'd miss it."

"I will miss everything once they pin Loretta's death on me. And that prostitute?" I shake my head, afraid to verbalize the obvious. "I'm not being paranoid, Mace."

"I never said you were." And those are the most frightening words my brother has ever spoken. "I suggest we move quickly. The clock is ticking, and the minute hand is not in your favor."

"It never has been." I can't think of a single thing that has.

Slowly, ever so painfully, we're opening Simone's proverbial casket one creak at a time as the foul stench of the past permeates everything good about my life and smothers me once again in those dark, inescapable days that I'm forever trapped in.

My God, let me be wrong. Let this all be a mindfuck of a coincidence. Let there be nothing to see. Let us move on.

But deep down in my gut, I know better than that.

Seven

Email from Twokidcircus@bex.org:

Bram Woodley is one supreme specimen. Are you sure you can hold onto a man like that?

Ree

I've felt anger in my life. I've felt outright rage, but this bitch, this monster, whoever they are, has just taken my emotions to an entirely different plane. How dare they! How dare they tunnel into my life so abrasively, tucking their nose into my existence—opining about things they have no business in. Simply put, I have a psychotic on my hands.

My phone buzzes, and I'm momentarily pulled from my dizzying trance. It's a text from Lena. **Scones, hot coffee. Come over. It's time.**

My blood boils hotter than the armpit of hell. Adrenaline rockets through me once again, twice in the span of five minutes. It's enough to kill anyone, really. My body goes numb, and my cheeks flush with heat. I know what Lena is saying, but deep down, I cannot comprehend why. What devil in hell has gotten ahold of her sanity? Never mind that. I already know the answer.

The kids are in school. Afternoon has just crested. Bram is at work. His own temperament has been off-kilter these last few days, but nothing like my own. No sooner did that text infiltrate my inbox from the same demon who's been prying into my windows, but now I've got a bigger problem to contend with. That emailing witch thinks she can ruin my life? And I do believe it's a woman trying to ruin my sanity—but sadly, my mother just said *hold my beer*.

Without permission, my feet shuffle me to the door and across the street to Lena's clapboard wonder painted a bright turquoise in a row of neat and tidy white stucco homes all hoping to be more unassuming than the next.

Voices emanate from inside as I head up the porch. They sound jovial as outright laughter vibrates through the screen. I don't bother knocking. Instead, I head on inside. The living room is dark, the curtains still drawn behind the sofa. But the voices rise like happy helium balloons, coming from the kitchen. The din of dainty dishes tapping fills the air like a cymbal, teacups to saucers, fine china no doubt. My God, Lena has pulled out the finery as if the Queen of England had landed.

And then I hear her, clear and defined. My mother's voice as she talks fast-paced, high-pitched, laughter bursting through her words, and the room lights up again with cackles. Three voices intermarrying to create one raucous cry that pierces through the membrane I've been cocooned in for so long. My mother had torn any barriers that I might have put in place and stomped her way back into my world like Godzilla thrashing his way through Percy Bay.

I step lightly to the end of the room and peer into the kitchenette to find three bodies, Lena, Astrid with that poor hen she holds captive, and—my God, my eyes cannot comprehend what they're seeing.

My mother has always been a large woman, with a shock of dark hair that was mercilessly teased and rising above her head like a necrotic crown. Her eyes, a pale shade of blue, so ice cold could shear the skin off your bones and set your teeth on edge without so much of a word. Her form, her very being had the power to instill a sure level of fear in anyone, and just as ferocious as she was, she was far more manipulative. It was her charm and questionable wit that garnered her fistfuls of dollars on behalf of her contrived sickly daughters. Mommy, as she had us trained to call her far longer than would have been thought acceptable. Here she is, *Mommy* in the flesh. The beauty of her demented plan was that she had not only convinced the world that my sister and I were suffering immeasurably, she managed to convince us as well. Not an entirely impossible feat when you're being fed steady doses of sedatives, muscle relaxers, laxatives, on top of being nutritionally and sleep-deprived. She had molded us into exactly what she needed us to be. We were so close to that brass ring, the Make-A-Wish trip for Lena to Disneyworld. It was the one place my mother dreamed of. Other women lusted after men. My mother lusted after a mouse. Makes sense in retrospect. She was a rat to begin with.

But this—this startling new version of her has caught me off guard. They prattle on with their conversation without notice of my presence, but their words swim around me like slippery fish I cannot grasp.

It's her face, that new body, the hair. It cannot be. My mother has morphed from a beast into something somewhat respectable. Gone are the spare three hundred plus pounds she was hauling around and in its place is a svelte woman, a waist that is cinched a little tighter than my own. She's donned a pair of white jeans—*white* jeans, something that in my mother's muumuu heyday would have been sacrilegious for anyone to wear. A peach blouse shows off her tanned shoulders and makes my stomach drop. My mother looks like some hipster grandmother I might encounter at the pick-up line down at Richard E. Moss.

That rat's nest that once stood on her head like a warning to the rest of the society, beaconing out the fact that she was not stable, do not trust her, do not give her two hundred dollars so she can pass proverbial go has all but disappeared. Her hair is tame, longer in the back, a smooth silky dark chocolate, not the bat wing black she was saturating her mane with in those tortured days gone by. It softens her features, makes her almost amicable, a kinder, gentler version of the monster she once was. Her face looks younger, so much more youthful than she has ever been. Her eyes are pulled back a notch. Plastic surgery? Who would have thought my mother would bow to the god of vanity. There's a smattering of cosmetics enhancing her eyes, her cheeks neatly contoured and that hateful mouth of hers carefully blushed and glossed.

Her head turns my way as if her antennae had finally picked up on me.

"Aubree Loraine Van Lullen?" Her voice chimes out like a horrible rusted gong that hasn't stopped resonating for years. "Is that you?"

Astrid and Lena cease with their trembling cackles as all eyes feast on me, but my gaze never wavers from my mother's. She is very much like a rabid dog. You need to stare it down. Let it know who is boss lest it eat you when you least expect it.

I was wrong. My mother's greatest deception hadn't yet taken place. No. Not by a long shot. This right here, this prized and painted version of her, is her greatest deception by far. Her reinvention, the reincarnation of the beast she is has first and foremost fooled my sister.

"Ree?" Lena calls out like the traitor she is. "I have some coffee for you." My sister offers a frenetic nod. "Come." She calls to me like a stray dog she's trying to get to do the bidding. A monster luring a little girl into the van by way of candy.

I find myself floating into the kitchen, oblivious of my feet moving, oblivious to the fact I'm still breathing, and quite frankly shocked as hell that I haven't wrapped my fingers around my mother's neck and killed her for the hell of it.

Astrid bucks as if she just came to and found herself in a den of wolves, and she might have. "Ree, you never mentioned the fact you have an amazing mother. My own mother is nothing but a Negative Nelly. I would sell her for a dollar. That woman has never spoken a kind word about me. Can you believe it? Her own daughter. But from what I can see, your mother is certainly something special." She rises as if to leave.

"No, stay." I grip her by the arm and push her back into her seat with force without meaning to. My heart beats rabid as I take in my own mother in this close proximity. There's something jarring about it, unnatural, and I'm afraid I might pass out. It's that feeling you get when you see a corpse for the first time. In theory, you can't imagine you'd be horrified. Especially if you knew and loved them. But upon closer inspection, you realize that there is something morbidly wrong. That our bodies are nothing more than a casing and we are so far from who we think we are. It changes your perspective on living until you forget about it. Until you see the next corpse, and you're jarred at the sight once again because humans are hardwired by nature to never get used to some things. It's an innate fear utilized by a careful craftsmanship of the mind to alert us to the fact a corpse isn't something you would ever want to keep around, much like my mother.

"You must stay." My voice brightens a notch. I might be speaking to Astrid, the asshole who I am almost certain is out to destroy my sanity via those ridiculous emails. But at this odd juncture, she's become a life raft. "Finish your coffee, please." My mother's blood-let of a mouth twitches, and a thought hits me like a brick to the chest. What if my mother has put her up to this? What if my mother has woven her spell around Astrid far before this fateful day and she seeded her mind with creative ways to torment her daughter?

"Yes, my mother is something." I couldn't bring myself to echo the word *special*. A quick montage of all those years suffering at her hands plays through my mind like a black and white horror film, Lena and I force-fed spoonfuls of that horrible poison as children. First, the meds arrived in their liquid form. We were relieved to graduate to pills once we were older, the hunger pains we suffered through, the gnawing feeling that there was a cat trying to claw its way out of my belly. I will never forget the horror of being told there is nothing that you can eat that wouldn't kill you. The waifs we had become, victims of Auschwitz in our own home. My mother the Nazi who ran the concentration camp. The *outings* as she called them— my mother gleefully paraded us at her office parties, at the park during company picnics. We were on full display for all to see, our frail frames a prison cell. But how we watched those other children play, run on healthy legs, and indulge in their fast-food lunches that smelled divine. We were fed a steady diet of paste, some cheap dollar store oatmeal, plain as paper, whose sole purpose was to keep us just this side of death. One day when my mother went to work, Lena picked the lock on the pantry and made us each a cup of ramen as she had seen our mother do for herself a hundred times. We didn't eat half of a single serving, splitting it between ourselves before we were full beyond measure. I vomited it into the toilet, and it tasted just as good coming back up. Lena and I partook in our little pantry heist for a solid month before my mother caught on. We had worked our way up to a single cup each, no vomiting, and it was our greed, our out-of-the-blue weight gain that was our undoing.

That bird in Astrid's arms lets out a howling cry and bats its wings as if its feet were on fire, and Astrid hops out of her seat, screaming and cursing up a storm.

That hairy chicken lunges for Lena as it hops right out of Astrid's arms, bouncing off my sister before ping-ponging through the room, landing on the table just shy of my mother.

My mother squawks, an angry primal beastly cry, and suddenly, I'm rooting for the bird.

"Get that thing the hell away from me," my mother's cries reverberate off the ceiling, and yet the bird is relentless in its pursuit.

Astrid dives over my mother in a full-bodied attempt to capture it, and the bird flaps its useless wings floating just enough to dig its talons into my mother's shoulder, then in another magnificent hop landing itself square on her head.

My mother freezes, as does all of time for one brief glorious moment, and I burst into laughter, a deep resonating cry of relief that permeates the infrastructure of this building and rides past the sky and into the stratosphere.

Astrid snatches the filthy bird off my mother, and both women look angrily toward me as if I had orchestrated the event.

Cosmic justice had allowed me to be here at just the right moment to witness the comical scene.

Astrid's entire chest caves in with a sigh. "I'd best get Rocky home. He's had a big day."

Lena nods to me and mouths the words *Big day?*

I can't help but scowl back at her. How dare she do something that would have been so private and normal for us just a moment before my mother crawled back into our lives? How dare she try to pretend that none of this happened? The grievance of reintroducing our mother back into the fold was far too much. We can never go back. It's impossible from my end.

Astrid takes off without a word from any of us, and it's just the original three in the room. Together again in a confined space just the way my mother liked it all those years ago. We never belonged to the world. We were her possessions to do with as she pleased.

She waddles toward me, her gait too ingrained in her cellular code to change with the mere drop of a dress size, her eyes set in a daze dead to mine. "You laughed at me."

I take a moment to marvel at the fact she still walks as if she weighs four hundred pounds. Old habits die hard, as does my hatred for her.

"I laughed at you." I nod, my own gaze just as hypnotic as it sits over hers. Her icy stare, that cold veneer, the evil percolating just beneath the surface—it's all there, palpable as ever. "I'm still laughing at you. The weight loss, the hair, the new face. None of it is an improvement. You are a walking, talking *lie*. And whatever you've told Lena is merely a manipulation to get back in our lives. To get back in control. It's not happening. Not with me. Not with Lena.

You may have her fooled for now, but it won't last long. You are a danger to yourself and others. I know what you are capable of. I know what you are doing—what you're still doing." I needle hard into her with those words. A part of me didn't want to come out and say anything about those emails. It would only enable her the right to deny them, strip me of my superiority of knowing she's behind them no matter who is actually pushing send. If I suspected it before I saw her, I can be certain of it now that she's here.

"I'm not just here for you, Aubree. I'm not just here for Lena. I've changed my life." Her left eye comes shy of winking, and a dull laugh pumps from me. Not even her own body could go along with the lie. "I'm here for my grandchildren."

A primal cry sails from my throat as I lunge at her, knocking her back to the pantry as my hands dig into her flimsy flesh, my fingernails carving right in soft as bread dough.

"Ree!" Lena snatches at my shirt to drag me away, her own fingernails clawing at skin, at the belt loop of my jeans until she manages to pluck me off her and I stagger backwards a few steps, panting as I struggle to catch my breath. "She means it. She's not the same. You need to give her a chance."

I look to my sister, who stands there exasperated, frustrated, at her wits' end with me of all people.

"What made you change your mind about her?" There has to be a valid reason. There is something at play other than my mother's goodwill, her bullshit excuse of an *I'm sorry*. Lena is no idiot. I know deep down she shares the same hatred for our mother as I do.

Lena's eyes round out as if she were plotting the words to put together and came up short.

"You don't have any good reason, Lena. Throw her back on the street and we can be sisters again. This is your moment. It's her or me."

The three of us pant relentlessly as the sound of our breathing clots up the space around us.

Sometimes you don't need any words at all to hear the remainder of the story.

"Oh. Lena," it comes out sorrowful, full of grief. I glance back to the beast who bore me. "Stay away from my children or I'll initiate a restraining order." I look to

Lena. "Same goes for you."

I head out and don't look back.

Eight

Bram

Erwin Wilson is a sad looking creature who once had the ability to frighten innocent people with his menacing tall frame, his natural muscular build. He was a homeless vagrant for years in the downtown district of Kaswell, a mere hop, skip, and hammer's blow from my former residence. But prison life, one might say, agrees with him. Gone is the layered grime that gave him an otherworldly glow of despair. His trash can meals have been replaced with powdered eggs and potatoes made fresh and hot daily. Chemically subdued are the inner voices and active hallucinations. In place of his scraggly mane, his hair has been shorn a tame two inches off his scalp. The holey scraps he once wore, layered like armor, an entire closet of despair all at once had vanished, and in its place a bright blue jumpsuit that brings out the cerulean hue in his eyes. Yes, you might say the three hots and a cot life is agreeing with Erwin Wilson very, very much.

It was Mason who garnered us clearance to visit Erwin on such short notice. Mason is a licensed private detective in New York and now in Maine and has been for as long as my life has warranted the effort. It's an odd thing to have shaped your brother's future by way of your own screwed-up existence, but that is what has landed this man, the one I called a monster for many, many years before us.

Erwin folds and refolds his hands. His eyes flit from Mason to me, unsure of what this visit entails. He's been briefed on who we are, and he offered a prolonged nod my way as if he understood my intimate relation to the woman he's doing time for killing. He should know me well. I sat in that courtroom like a dutiful husband. I had patted myself on the back for helping to put him away. Mason bought me a beer afterwards to celebrate.

"How are you?" I go with something benign. An icebreaker that works in most every situation but this one, I suppose. If I were in prison, doing fifty to life, the answer would always be *shitty*.

He lifts his chin, a move that almost looks scholarly

on him. "I'm good, Peter. And you?"

Something inside of me flinches when he says my name so boldly. But it came out frank and honest, and suddenly, it feels as if we're visiting a long-forgotten uncle instead of the man who slaughtered my wife. And that is the primary reason for our visit. One last turning of the stone to see if we've left anything undiscovered. My gut has been churning for the last few days because I am certain as hell we have left a lot of damned things undiscovered.

I glance to Mason, unsure of how to dive in. I'm positive Erwin Wilson does not care how I am doing. He maintained his innocence all through the trial. But the fact he was covered in my wife's DNA, the murder weapon tucked hastily in his jacket, did not bode well for him.

Mason clears his throat, then flashes that warm, welcoming smile that could make the strongest believer hand over his soul. Yes, Mace can be a devil when he has to, and for me, he will wear those horns twenty-four seven. I do appreciate all he's done for me. If there were a decent way to pay him back, I would have done it by now.

"Erwin"—Mason starts—"we know you'd like to put

the case behind you. As would we." He tips his head my way as if I were just an aside. "You do look good, by the way. I'm glad about that."

"Me too." I decide to jump in, both feet. "Erwin, tell me exactly what you think happened that day. How did you get from Kaswell to Lake Glen?" I already know every detail of his story, but I've let his words collect dust in the recesses of my mind, and it's time for a good buff and polish.

His jaw moves from side to side as if he were chewing on his thoughts, literally. There is something methodical about Erwin I had not seen before. But I was filled with rage back then. I only saw what I wanted to, and what I saw was a very guilty bastard. And yet ironically, and I'm ashamed to admit it, I had a touch of relief once Simone passed away, and to this day I'm not sure why. Life kept folding in on itself, one nightmare after the next. I had fully expected to meet with an untimely demise myself. Part of me still waits for my own proverbial hammer to drop.

He takes in a full breath, sniffing hard like a coke fiend. The pale backdrop of the room behind him makes him stand out like a shadow, a negative of himself. That's what happens when you stare at something for too long while the sun casts its fury behind it. It burns the image into your mind, and you can see the impression of it long after you've closed your eyes. Something tells me I will see this new version of this once monster in my sleep. I had before. Only this time I will see him as a frail old man—a softer version, sanitized of all the rage I funneled his way. There is no more rage left inside of me for Erwin because I realize how powerless he really is. All of my rage is shiny and new for whoever is clawing at the back door of my life, demanding entry the most frightening way of all, through my mind.

"I was told it was a Tuesday."

My stomach tightens, and I try not to look at my brother. As much as I hate the fact that Erwin began his diatribe with hearsay, I understand how needless it is to remember which day of the week it is when your life is turned upside down.

"I had just finished up my work for the day"—he continues—"I felt uneasy. No voices that afternoon or evening, though, and that might be why I felt so uneasy." His chest bounces with a chuckle. "Camden House was taking care of me. Gave me meds each damned afternoon." Camden House is a halfway house that volunteers its resources to helping identify the homeless and aid the mentally ill with medication if need be. They corroborated this part of his story. What they could not confirm was whether or not he was *cheeking* those meds. Not an uncommon practice among the mentally ill. In fact, rumor has it that all of those "voices" frown upon imbibing the best that modern medicine has to offer. It's unclear how lucid he really was that day. Thus, his testimony is more than questionable.

"Go on," I prod. My stomach is lightly growling. It's almost time for my next meal, and God knows this entire experience is beginning to exhaust me. I used to chide Simone that she wore me out. And here she's been dead for close to a decade and she's still wearing me out just the same. Deep down, I damn her for that. It doesn't bode well for the poor widower to think darkly of his long-deceased spouse, especially not after the bludgeoning that took place. But Simone wasn't your average beloved spouse. She was so much more, a well that ran too deep, too dark. I can see her eyes piercing me with their hypnotic stare.

You are my everything, she would repeat for years. It was her choral lament. But it never came out with kindness. Simone had a way of shrouding each of her words in a veiled threat.

Erwin picks at his left nostril. "So I don't think I saw the Camden people that day because the car they sent to pick me up came a little earlier than that."

There is that nebulous *they* once again. If you simply popped into the conversation, one might assume that he was talking about the Camden people themselves, but I didn't just pop into the conversation. I've been listening in for years. The legal system, however, concluded there was no "they". That there was no car. Erwin took a bus to Madrano Heights, the neighborhood just below ours, and hoofed it the rest of the way. Uphill—a steep hill at that. It would have been exhausting, considering all of the clothes he had on that day, dirt encrusted jackets, two pairs of jeans. That was the one element of the story that has always bothered me. In fact, I walked it a few weeks later, granted in the heat of the day, but I was wheezing by the time I made it back to the house, back to the crime scene. But this old man had the energy to bash my wife's face in within an inch of his life, and, of course, all of her life was spent in the effort.

Mason leans in, letting out a sigh that sums up everything. "What kind of car was it again? What did the person look like?"

"Small car. Hell, I don't know if it was a man or woman or what they looked like. It was dark. I went for a ride. They gave me a beer out of the deal."

Mason lifts a brow my way. There was a beer missing from the fridge. I only know this because I was down to three that morning. It's the kind of things men notice when it's the only thing keeping them going. My kids were dead. My career wasn't important. I was still grieving, reeling. And that's why I went fishing. An overnight trip that I will forever live to regret.

Mace wraps his knuckles over the table as if calling him back to attention. Although, he might have been calling me. I can't seem to get my mind to sit still, not here, not ever.

"And when you got to the house, what happened?"

"I opened the door and went inside like I was told to do."

Here is where that nebulous "they" come into play again. Erwin was told to do many things that night.

He cocks his head as if considering this. "I went into the kitchen and got the damn beer myself. Had an opener in my pocket. You never know when something like that will come in handy."

"And my wife?" I interject. "What was she doing at the time?"

He purses his lips, his eyes slit to nothing as he takes me in through those seething slits. Erwin has never appreciated the fact that I've accused him of such a heinous crime. He was prosecuted by the state, but his crooked finger always seems to point right back at me for landing him in the predicament he's in. And in a way, it *was* my fault. I had married that woman who was killed. Had those kids who had drowned. I had started this nightmare, someway, somehow. It feels comfortable to bear the blame. That woman and those children were my charges, and somewhere along the line I fucked it all up. I couldn't keep anyone alive or safe, with the exception of myself. I'll be dammed if I'm going to screw it all up a second time. Ree and the kids come to mind, and my chest bucks with emotion as I do my best to stifle it.

"I never saw your wife, Peter. I got the beer and left. When I got dropped back off, they shoved a parting gift my way. I didn't notice the blood. Just put the damn thing in my pocket. A hammer is hard to come by where I lived, but a good accessory to have with you in case the wrong people come around."

I sag in my seat, trying to absorb it all once again. It's almost comical listening to him talk about the wrong people as if there were monsters bigger than him he needed to shield himself from. But my gut is still clenched as if I were waiting for more.

"Try to think back and see if you can remember anything new. Anything at all that might trigger a memory of that night. Did the person who, you say, drove you around have any jewelry on, or an accent, maybe painted fingernails or a tattoo?"

He shakes his head, that faraway look in his eyes lets me know he's rewinding time.

Mace leans in. "How about the car? Was there an odor when you got in? Did they play music? Hell, I don't know, did it have dirty windows?"

My brother is grappling for straws, and to see him so exasperated makes this effort feel like a big, giant waste.

Erwin tips his head back abruptly as if he were just slapped in the face. "Yes, there was something, something silly. A tiny sticker of an armadillo. I grew up in New Mexico, and I remember thinking now there's something you don't see in the city. I thought, here I have one thing to be grateful about. Armadillo-free living." His expression sours because, as it turned out, there was nothing for him to be grateful about whatsoever.

I look to Mace, and then like a celestial hammer from the sky it hits us both at once.

"Shit," I hiss.

Mace offers a covert nod my way as we wrap it up with Erwin. I go as far as shaking the old man's hand and about knock him to the floor with shock over it.

Mace and I wait until we're outside of the prison before pausing, our faces stone-cold with fury for not extricating that little seemingly unimportant detail from him earlier.

"I say we head over to Armadillo Rental and see how far back they keep their records." He gives my arm a quick squeeze. "I hate to say it, little brother, but Simone may never have gotten the justice we thought we gave her."

A thousand insane scenarios rotate through my mind, none of them too sorry for Simone's lack of justice.

"If he's right, someone drove him to the murder scene, smeared his DNA over just enough of the house to put him away, and trucked him back to his street corner with the murder weapon."

"Shit," Mason barks as he kicks a loose stone into the landscaping.

"You don't get to get angry," I seethe and I pull him in by the sleeve. "We don't kick anything. More importantly, we don't kick ourselves." My heart strums wildly in my chest. "If we've been set up—if he's been set up—then this thing, this spider's web I found my way into all those years ago—it's not over. That body at the fundraiser, Loretta." My eyes search the barbed wired field to my right as if searching for answers. "It means—"

"It means the spider is finally ready for its meal. Maybe the others were simply appetizers."

I look to Mace, my eyes hypnotically trained to his. Ever since our father took off, there has been a cloud of foreboding in our lives. It grew far more ominous, turned black as night when my children, my wife died. And it has never cleared. Instead, it crouches lower, looms right over my head, pregnant with fury, ready to unleash the final fury of hell as if this were what it was gathering strength for all along. I can practically hear the thunder roll, growling in the distance, drumming through time and space as it makes its way closer, prowling along the periphery of my life as it lets out a deafening roar that paralyzes me from breathing.

The sky of my misfortune is black as night.

And something tells me it is about to rain like hell.

There's no running from the impending storm. Something tells me I'll have to face it head-on. And unfortunately for my family, so will they.

Nine

Ree

An icy wind blew in from the north, and I became a creature in hiding. The kids went to school, and I went right back into my curtain drawn home. There was a blistering pain in the depths of my heart when I drove by Lena's house. It felt like I was subjecting myself to a nuclear heat to look over at it. I could feel my soul trying to evict itself from my body. This was a new prison my mother had put me in. I had thought that getting away from her, out of her clutches would have satiated my desire for freedom, but just her presence, her thick evil, less than a hundred yards from my person lets me know that she can put me in a prison whenever she damn well pleases, and judging by the fact she's here, she damn well pleases.

Lena is at work, I know this. Therefore, I can deduce my mother is bolting from window to window like a feral cat trying to escape its suburban hell, waiting, watching to see what kind of a viral reaction she's sponsored from me—garnering the meat for her next ridiculous email. I thought she might be pulling the puppet strings with Astrid, and now I'm beginning to think this is wickedness straight from the nectar. Of course, it's her. She specializes in psychological torment. And as much as I was shocked to see Astrid buddying up to her, it pleased me in a sick way. She should be heavily exposed to my mother's brand of psychosis. If she is very, very lucky, she will receive a full dose of her affection. Ultimately, everyone my mother's necrosis touches dies a slow death. My mother in effect is the Grim Reaper, or in the least his right-hand man. A demonic entity in and of herself, who has mastered the skill of killing people long before they ever die. She is an ardent believer in suffering. She bows at the altar of misery and sacrifices pure souls to the cause each day. She is a purveyor of grief, a waking nightmare, a heated poker ready to strike anyone and everyone in her vicinity.

Bram was up early today. He had a restless night of sleep, while I wrestled it out with my nightmares right there next to him. He dotted my lips with a kiss before leaving, and I inhaled his cologne deeply as if it was medicine. Bram is the balm that can heal all of the wounds my mother ripped open yesterday. And, believe me, I find Lena just as culpable.

The spring sky is dove-gray and rife with misery. An ominous gloom has come to Percy Bay. A sure sign of foreboding, an omen trying to warn the residents of my mother the plague.

I make a cup of coffee—black, no sugar. I need to taste the bitterness, feel the burn—a literal palate cleanse to scrub the wickedness I inadvertently inhaled yesterday from my cellular structure.

Try as I might, I cannot put my mother out of my mind. I see her everywhere, drifting before me like a ghost, my reflection in the mirror—now that she's melted away to nothing, the resemblance is horrifically uncanny. I see her floating there in my coffee as I stare at the dark water and taste her bitterness on my tongue. And that's when the truth hits me, the building smashing over my spirit. There is no refuge from her. The earth is not big enough. There is nowhere left to run and hide. Her wings have the ability to darken every corner of this planet. But there is one thing that might be the panacea, and tragically, it's my morbid fascination with my husband's brutally murdered first wife. She is the one person who might be willing to swap places with me. Trading my mother for all those hammer blows she endured would seem obvious to the untrained eye. But my mother is just as lethal as a hammer. I should know. She's been bludgeoning me for years.

Death would be quicker, Simone, and if it weren't for my children, the husband we share, I would crave this, too.

I drag my coffee, my phone, and my striking resemblance to this newer version of the woman who bore me upstairs and to my closet. I don't even bother slogging her notebooks to the bed anymore. Instead, I sit on a pillow on the floor, my coffee nestled next to a pair of high-heeled boots I haven't worn in years, and I pull out the old composition book, riffling through it furiously as if it were a novel I couldn't wait to finish in haste. The thought of finishing them invokes a sense of dread in me almost as deep as the one my mother is capable of inflicting.

I've grown to care about Simone. Her insecurities

have become my own. Her hunger for life is contagious. I'd like to think that in some other lifetime we would have been friends. Good friends. Our children would have been siblings. I'm more than slightly infatuated with that bubbly, full of life redhead my husband once had everything with.

How could Bram be so ridiculous as to step out on her? After thinking about it for some time, I've determined that she's misinterpreted the situation. Bram wouldn't dare cheat on her, would he? Simone was vivacious, the mother of his children, so gorgeous she could have walked every runway in New York and Europe.

Before I was exposed to this intimate side of Simone, a small part of me used to believe that Bram had found in me someone younger than his previous wife, full of my own youthful innocence and natural curiosity that would invigorate his world. A small part of me believed that I offered him things that she couldn't. That not only did I rescue him from his grief, but that I was a shiny new toy on a silver platter, something akin to a trophy wife upgrade. And here, after spending mere hours with the inner workings of Simone's deepest thoughts, I can see I was nothing but a downgrade.

May 25th

Peter came home two days ago acting as if nothing had ever happened. As if his penis hadn't just invaded some other woman's vagina. He showered and changed, watched television with the kids, and had the nerve to call me a party pooper when I didn't want to join them.

That night he accused me of sulking. Sulking! I wanted to laugh in his face. How dare he waltz back in here, having satiated his every dark desire, and expect everything to remain status quo at home.

Of course, he doesn't know that I'm apprised of his dalliance. How frightening to think this is the way he always behaves when he comes home from the city. And to think I've played the role of "happy wifey" so perfectly before. I was right there with him, watching endless Disney movies on a loop. Ushering the kids to bed early so I could do my best to seduce my husband. And how ridiculously exhausted he would come home to us. Come to think of it, he never fell victim to my advances, always sighting his unusual fatigue.

Ha! No wonder he was so exhausted. He just came back from a marathon fuck-fest with who knows who for who knows how long. It's a wonder he could get it up at all for me. I am the boring wife after all who offers up nothing but mundane sex, who forces him to live a desperately vanilla missionary position life, who bitches at him for not helping with the dishes, or meals, who nags endlessly at him to put up curtain rods, to fix the broken showerhead in the guest bathroom, to take the damned hammock out of the box and put it together so I can nap in the sun, blissfully unaware while he finds someone to suck his dick in New York.

Thank you, Peter, for redefining my life for me in such an amazingly (boring) way. I have been relegated to the bottom shelf, stored in a banker's box collecting dust in the dark recesses of your heart.

Do you have a heart, Peter? I'm not so sure anymore. You make me feel as if I've gone the way of newspapers and you've moved on to digital, something far more faster, accurate, and urgent to scratch that itch between your legs.

Is she better in bed or just different? Or is it something basic, like the fact she's simply not me? I get it. Men are hardwired that way. My own father cheated on my mother once. Of course, my mother, being the magnificent shrew she is, taught him a lesson he would never forget.

Perhaps that would be best. No messy divorce. No splitting the children between us. I am not a vase you get to smash against the wall when you don't feel like using me anymore, once I've lost my appeal. Does my belly sag too much for you? Too damn bad. I bore you two children with a third growing blissfully inside me. That's right, Peter. You've got your dirty secret, and I have mine—something pure and right that you are so willing to throw away for something reckless in New York. I have news for you, Peter. I haven't gone out of fashion. I'm not done on this earth, and neither are our children. But once I'm done with the little lesson I'm about to set out—the only one who will be done will be you and that whore you cling to.

My heart pounds heavy against my chest as I reach for my coffee with a strangulating grip.

Simone was pissed and rightly so. And her poor mother. If Simone was apprised of her father's indiscretion, then she certainly lived through that pain once. My own heart aches for her. Bram would never do that to me, would he? There is no possibility he's hardwired that way.

All of those late-night meetings he's been having with his brother come crashing to the forefront of my mind, and my heart lurches right up into my throat.

No. Couldn't be. My Peter—Bram, he's different. There isn't even a lot of room in my heart to believe he did that to Simone. She must have seen someone who looked like Bram from behind. That's the only logical explanation. Simone was hiding a pregnancy from him. Her hormones were going nuclear. Of course, her mind skipped to the bawdiest conclusion.

My hands warm over the covers of the journal as if it was her skin and carefully I peel it open once again.

May 27th

They say you can never truly know anyone outside of yourself and that even you are a mystery to your own person half of the time. What I stumbled upon this afternoon has eviscerated everything I thought I knew about Peter, about me, about who we really are. I've taken to putting you (my sweet salvation of a friend) in a lockbox. I've contacted my sister and shared my suspicions. She's in

Norway for work (traveling PR slut that she is) but promised to be back stateside soon to help me work through this.

I'm afraid I can't wait. I'm afraid that I'm in danger. The kids are my first priority, of course, and I will watch them like a hawk. I'm ready to fire Kelly. Her incompetence is showing, a weak crack in the armor like that can cost us our lives. I need to figure out a way to move money from one bank account to another without arousing suspicion from Peter. I went online to some abused spouse forum and found that the best way to move money was to purchase gift cards from the grocery store. I can use them later to survive, then buy the kids clothing and shoes. My God, I'll have to get a real job, interfacing with real people, and we both know how much I loathe people. That was not intended to be funny, but I can feel you laughing.

I can't fathom moving from this beautiful house—our home. I won't be able to contact the police until I have everything settled. But that poor girl. Strangulation is such a terrible way to die. How horrific to take a life. They'll find him. And if they don't, he's given me the evidence to put him away for good. It's in his shed—my God, Peter has *always needed that stupid shed and for what? For the gardening tools he never uses? For that old dusty mower? We have a gardener. The signs were all there. So plain as the nose on my face. Help me, God. Help me survive this nightmare and bring my children to safety. I will spend the entire day trying to figure out best how to pursue this. Kelly will be with the kids and me at the lake. I'll need her more than ever.*

May 27th. That's a day that will forever live in infamy. I turn the next few pages, but they're all blank. I knew they would be. Simone lost two vital pieces of her heart that day. A horrible irony, considering she was readying to leave her Peter.

Tears roll down my cheeks, falling hot over my knees. I flip the sturdy book to the end, and two small newspaper clippings fall out. Newspaper. I can't help but find the irony in that, too. The paper is yellowed around the edges, and as I turn one over, I see Isla and Henry staring back at me, expressive smiles, blushed cheeks, so full of life. I offer a weak smile right back at them. I wish they were still here. Lilly and Jack would love them. But would there be a Lilly and Jack? What exactly did Simone have on Peter? It all sounded so very cryptic. Who strangled the whore from New York? Surely she didn't really think Peter was capable of such a crime. He's hardly capable of sleeping outside of the bounds of the bedroom. As much as I love Peter—Bram, he is very missionary position in all areas of life, to borrow the analogy from Simone.

The second article slips into my fingers as if biding for attention, and I turn it over, my eyes glossing quickly over the words, manically eating them up while my insides do a revolution.

Dear God, no.

Ten

Bram

Armadillo Car Rental protects their customers' privacy to a level that makes the White House security team look like a rent-a-cop situation from the mall.

Mason has traveled to the heart of Kaswell, to the exact location that we believe the rental car may have come from, and spoken to, bribed, and casually threatened each of their four eager-to-serve-and-protect employees. One thing we know for certain, the car was most likely rented on or around August second and returned the next day. A small gray sedan that couldn't have tripped more than forty miles if it was a clean round trip.

After a long day at the office, rife with routine drillings, fillings, a crown, and an ornery senior in his eighties who informed me that dentistry was nothing more than modern-day train robbing—on behalf of his uninsured granddaughter with a mouthful of chalk for teeth—I close the door to my office and pull a thin silver laptop out of my briefcase. It feels as if I pulled Simone right back into the land of the living. I set it on my desk and examine it like some scientific artifact. It indeed feels like one, some relic from a painful time best forgotten. I pluck the cords out and fire it up, open the monitor with caution as if I was opening a crypt, some horrible time capsule that threatens to rip those measly emotional scabs right off and cause me to finally bleed to death the way God intended.

The screen blinks to life, and my chest bucks, anticipating the worst. A happy family stares back at me, our nuclear family unit set as the screensaver, but the screen goes black and a thin gray window prompts me to put in a password.

After the great tragedy that had stolen our lives, and, yes, I count myself in that number along with my children and wife, I had to slowly go about the task of removing their material imprint from this planet. For almost six weeks after Simone was bludgeoned to death, the house remained a crime scene. Neighbors moved overnight to avoid the media circus, to avoid the *killer* on the loose. Once I had custody of the house again, the coroner gave me the name of a cleanup committee dedicated to scraping brains off ceilings. Every trace of Simone's DNA was excavated to the tune of four thousand dollars. It was a nightmare that appeared to be subsiding to the untrained eye, but the truth of it was, I didn't want any part of that house ever again. Simone and I hadn't even gotten to the task of clearing out the kids' rooms. They were in full-on shrine mode, and I was content with that. It was where I spent most of my time after the funerals. Twin caskets. Twin agonies that never ceased. In a way, it was a relief knowing that the house was tainted, that I could never go back. After the DNA scraping team finished, I had the carpet ripped out and hired another crew to go in and pick the living room of all its contents. I called in a dumpster, threw out the bloodstained furniture, and was left with yet another gaping hole in my life—a minuscule one at that in comparison to all the other holes, but my life had enough holes in it that you could drive a Semi through.

My fingers tap over the keyboard, and my heart thumps unnaturally. I hadn't opened the laptop since that day, let alone touched the very places my wife's hands last happily danced away. But the pictures, all of the pictures of the kids were carefully loaded and sent God knows where through this device by my very careful wife who was excellent at documenting our journey together. I try one password, then another, the kids' names, our names, but it's not until I try the kids' names in combination does the screensaver blink to life, the four of us on the lake in a tiny skiff I had rented, a life jacket on both Henry and Isla. Henry's expressive eyes look as if they're reaching out to me, calling for help from the other side of the screen, from the other side in general. And my hand slaps over my mouth to absorb some of the pain.

Isla. Beautiful, sweet Isla with her quirky smile, her tongue poking through the hole between her teeth. She always had a joke at the ready, a silly knock-knock joke that she read in a book she borrowed from the library. She had a dark laugh she expressed frequently while tormenting her brother. They were best friends. The only small comfort to be gleaned in that great tragedy is that they were together. And yet when Simone died, there was little comfort to know the three of them were reunited. To lose a wife so tragically after losing both children so horrifically, it didn't make sense. It boggled my mind to think about. God knows I couldn't process it. I'm not sure why this happened. But deep down, I suspected my sins had come home to roost.

Loretta comes to mind, her body lying at the base of that hotel room, her limbs set out in jagged angles, and I quickly blink her out.

The rest of the desktop is littered with pictures of the kids, memes she's stolen from the Internet, inspirational phrases which I have always found odd coming from a woman who denied anything to do with spirituality. Her own thoughts about death never amounted to more than the fact she believed we turned into compost. No soul, no spirit, no heavenly choir to welcome us home. I certainly hope she's discovered she was wrong—that she's holding the children close to her heart right at this very moment.

I head over to the documents folder but find it empty and mull that fact over for a second. Simone wrote as voraciously as she read. She had folders for each one of her projects, and I used to marvel at how many plates she had spinning at once.

I click over to finder and check out the apps, the software, all of it set to bare bones, basic as if the laptop never belonged to her for four years. I click onto the Internet and look up her history, but there's nothing. My stomach cinches. The laptop was closed and left on the bed. An action that I thought was odd to begin with, considering Simone never sat and watched television without doing something with her hands and usually that involved her laptop and her phone. If Simone was anything, she was the queen of multitasking.

I run a quick search of the security, the laptop history and find nothing. I head back into the desktop and click into each of the dozens of pictures littering the screen as microscopic thumbnails. Isla and Henry, Simone in most of the shots. Their eyes. Their smiles. It kills me on every level.

My fingers tap over the keys faster and faster, and a nauseating pattern begins to emerge. In every one of these pictures the kids, Simone, they're all in their bathing suits. Simone was able to be in a few because Kelly was taking them. The lake is visible behind them. That damned lake.

My heart stops cold when I see that pink ribbon tied to Isla's ponytail. It was still in her hair when I saw her later that night at the morgue.

A bite of acid tears at my stomach, and I hold my breath as I click through them faster and faster. Simone with the kids, waving to the kids from shore, a shot of her walking away, and it gives off an eerie voyeuristic feel. Back to the kids in full splash mode, a couple of the ground, a shot of a pale leg in that final shot, Simone's. I inspect it further. The foot is coming toward the camera. I think on this for a second. Simone said she was busy writing, and I'm assuming that's where she was off to. She probably came back to collect the camera from Kelly before she left.

I pull out my phone to text Mace my findings. He was the one that suggested I check it out in the event there was something I missed.

Laptop seems to be picked clean. The only evidence that it belonged to Simone are the pictures. No articles, no projects. Would that just disappear over time? I already know the answer to it, but a part of me still hits send.

He texts right back. **No. Do you think it was sanitized?**

I glare up over at the laptop and spot Simone's

smiling face, and it suddenly feels like she's laughing.

Why would she do that? What would she have to hide?

He texts back. **Don't know. But I got my hands on the records for Armadillo Rental Cars on and around the dates of the crime. You're welcome.**

"Shit." I sit up and stare at the phone a good long while. **I'll meet you at the Thirsty Fox in an hour.**

Make it two. I've got another fish to fry. See you there.

Two hours. My heart thumps wildly in my chest as I look back at that screensaver, a painful reminder of another life, another wife, another beautiful, beautiful set of children.

I pull it forward and get online. I head over to Facebook to her personal page. The last post was a meme, a woman in hair rollers complaining about it being a man's world while she holds a globe under her bare foot, a baby in the other. I've seen it a thousand times, but I force myself to look at the image until my eyes burn.

All Simone and I ever did was argue. After the kids passed away, we cried but not together, not mostly.

Simone was so full of toxic rage, so much negativity. I couldn't look at her the right way without sparking a fury in her.

The image of the meme flips into one of those forefront background images, and I see something in it I've never seen before. Partially hidden behind her is a man with a woman's legs wrapped around his back. The woman looks young and fit, a wash of blond hair dangling from the side. The woman in the rollers seems oblivious to the fact her husband is cheating on her. Is that what this is? Why would she post this? My ears thump with their own heartbeat.

I scroll down and read the comments, some as recent as four months ago.

I'm so sorry this has happened to you. You've been through so much. I hope he gets the death penalty.

Cut his dick off!

Let me kill him. I'll pay my way there and back.

You and your beautiful children are on my heart. Please, authorities, if you are reading this, reopen the investigation on those beautiful babies. The parents said they were strong swimmers. Strong swimmers do not just drown in a calm lake. People have reported hearing no screaming. I know that drowning is very quiet, but there would have been splashing at least! Somebody do something. The husband is guilty, and he will do this again. He is out for blood!

Saw the bastard on TV last night. You don't need to be a body language expert to know he's lying. He did it. And he's gonna get away with it because the police are too damned incompetent to do anything about it.

BURN IN HELL Peter Woodley!!!

It's that last comment I relate to the most. I most certainly have been burning in hell. A silent inferno enveloped me the day Isla and Henry died. I was in a dense fog right up until Simone died. Baptized with gasoline and it only enraged the flames.

It's all been hell. My world has never stopped burning. I scroll down to the rest of Simone's posts, pictures of our children—I've memorized them all, but those smiles sing out in my mind like my ol' favorite song. Simone smiling, so happy, so perfectly beautiful in her own right, and even so the sight of her clenches my stomach, brings back all of those negative vibes she put there to begin with. Simone was a briar patch in scorching heat, and Ree is a poppy field on a comfortable day. We wouldn't have made it. I would have had joint custody of our children, and she would have undoubtedly made a career out of poisoning them and the world against me. I should never have strayed. I should have walked into a lawyer's office. Not a hotel room. I should have thought it through with my bigger head, not buried it between the thighs of some poor woman. Loretta, who, too, was brutally murdered.

A vat of acid explodes inside the pit of my stomach. My flames are contagious. I have burned so many worlds to the ground, I should be imprisoned for the safety of others.

I scroll down even farther, down past the season of pain. I watch the dates, a demonic timestamp of the downfall of my being.

A flicker of a sad smile comes and goes.

Past the memes and general updates about the minutia of life a post catches me off guard.

I lean in to get a better look at what my wife had to say, and my heart stops cold.

Eleven

Email from Twokidcircus@bex.org:

You were bought with a price. You are not your own.

Ree

Lilly and Jack are the true pure lights shining bright in my world. They twirl and laugh in the yard as I sit and watch at the patio table, a warm meal already in their bellies. I stopped off at the Hungry Burger on the way home, drive–thru. There will be no warm meal waiting for Bram—Peter, whoever the hell he might be. I'm hurt and I'm comfortable nurturing my anger.

My hand moves absentmindedly to my belly. Could I have a new life brewing in my belly the same way that Simone did just moments before her life fell apart? I wonder if she ever told him? Even if she did, he might not remember it. He confessed that everything after the kids died felt like a nightmare, a waking living hell and his mind didn't work the same after that.

He couldn't remember the days of the week, and whether or not he had remembered to eat was a question mark. Everything was happening and nothing would stick. A part of me wants to disavow Simone's news clipping and what it might mean. Dismiss it as evidence of a paranoid woman who lost her mind after her children were taken so horrifically from her. I can't imagine the horror. One minute they are playing, laughing, filling the air with their happy-go-lucky squeals, and the next dead silence. Twin bodies lying motionless, facedown, asleep like dolls. Only God knows what happened. I've read reports. I've read everything about them. After Bram and I met that first night, I went home and did my due diligence, combed through a plethora of archived information on the Internet. I Googled the shit out of them. Early on, the armchair sleuths determined that one of the twins lost his or her footing, maybe he or she had gotten a cramp and panicked, and the other drowned in an effort to help. They say that's common, a drowning man often takes down his rescuer. Unless you have a floatation device to help them, you will become one. As terrible as it would be not to help the one begging for mercy, you have to go into the situation knowing it might just be your last day yet. They think it was Henry who was in trouble. Maybe asthma, maybe it was a game gone wrong, sibling rivalry, demonic possession. The Internet was rife with all kinds of theories. But I did think of Simone, even on that first day that I met Bram. How colorful and perfect her life was up until that fated moment. You could scroll through her social media and feel you really knew her when you were done. So cheery. Such an unmatched zest for life. She was living her best life with her best children, and the man she thought was her best husband until one tragedy begot the next. Terror upon terror. She was Job from the Bible, only she didn't get the happy ending. She got the hammer.

"Mommy!" Lilly comes over shrieking. "Jack won't share with me." She smacks her lips in a cute frenetic way that makes the sound of bubbles rising from under water, and my muscles freeze. Isla and Henry flash through my mind.

"Jack? Share or no video games." It's a lie, though. I'll need to keep them occupied tonight. Once Bram comes home, we have plenty of things to discuss.

Lilly speeds off and I'm left ruminating once again, the dizzy carousel of those haunting words. Three homeless prostitutes dead in New York during the same time frame Peter was stepping out on Simone. All of them with one of their fingers missing, same finger, pinky. Just like the woman that I found at the fundraiser that night. Just like the woman I heard about staying at the same hotel as Bram. Fingers as trophies for a madman.

"Knock, knock!" The cheerful cry of a female catches me off guard from behind.

My head turns so fast, breaking my neck is a real possibility, and I freeze solid once I spot her. All I see is red.

My mother, the newfound skeleton, is attempting to make a debut in my own backyard. I'm moved to snap her neck and dig a shallow grave to commemorate the event. If it weren't for the kids, I might have.

"Get out," my voice is low and guttural, the growl of a demon.

"Now, *now*." Her face configures into a painful looking grimace. She's lost so much weight there's nothing but loose skin everywhere you look. Maybe that's why she's back. She'd like to reinstate our old act—perhaps with my own children so she can get the money to snip her skin off. She has always been a waste of skin. I say they take it all off. Let her walk around this planet like the monster she is.

She falls into the seat next to me, and my adrenaline hits new heights. It's as if I've stepped out of my body. My own vocal cords betray me with their inability to perform. Can't breathe.

"You know, funny little story." She leans forward a bit as her eyes inspect the children. "Your Lilly is just as scrappy as you were. Looks as if someone rewound time about twenty years." Her tongue clicks against the roof of her mouth. "That Jack is all Bram. But that's not his real name, now is it?"

A chill runs through me. So many options on how to dispose of her body, so little time to analyze the situation.

I will kill my mother. I already know this. And then I will either frame my sister for it as punishment for hauling this witch back into our midst or I'll do away with her, too.

One of the many therapists I saw in the aftermath of my mother's original destruction suggested that I rid my life of toxic people. I think it's high time I take her advice.

"Aw, come on, Aubree girl."

A shiver runs through me when she calls me by that name. Aubree girl. I was her Aubree girl when she needed me to take those questionable meds. When she was holding my hair back while I puked my scant dinner into the toilet. While I wrung out my insides from the insane diarrhea she inflicted on me. I was her Aubree girl when she placed my feeble body in that wheelchair and paraded me around her coworkers, the local churches, anyone with a pocket.

"You know"— her hot pink nails claw at the table a moment, but her gaze remains pinned on the kids—"you were, and still are, my favorite. I don't know why, but Lena never could stand up in the same light. She was lost in your shadow, even in my own eyes. What a terrible thing for a mother to admit." A dull laugh pumps from her. "But it's us, alone. We can share secrets. So tell me, did he kill her? The wife. Simone, was it? How painful to have a hammer pounded over you. Rumor has it, they found bits and pieces of her sprayed all over that house. Read all about it as soon as Lena told me who he was."

My stomach churns. Bile burns the back of my throat

at the thought of Lena and my mother discussing my husband, *Simone*. Simone feels sacred to me, especially after reading her private thoughts, knowing her innermost secrets. Lena is officially dead to me. Simone is my new sister. A dead one, too. I seem to be collecting corpses these days, and soon enough my mother will up the number.

"You know what I don't get?" Her eyes dart in my direction briefly, and that fire brewing in my belly stokes ten times hotter. "Why in the world would you let that chicken girl get some alone time with your Peter? Anyone with eyes can see she's got the hots for him. Don't tell me I raised a fool. Aubree girl, you can see it, too. She told me all about those appointments they have in his office. His hands touching her mouth, stroking her tongue like he means it. You know what she said? She said she ran into him downtown and they had drinks one night. Imagine that! Your Peter and chicken woman. Now I don't know what happened next, but she made it sound like she had a fantastic time." She shakes her head, and Lilly looks over at the two of us with caution, inspecting this woman by my side as if she might be trouble. Lilly has always been a perceptive child.

My mother chortles before taking a breath. "Said she's filing for a legal separation from her husband. He doesn't understand her. He doesn't get the obsession with the birds. She's had enough. But, of course, that frees up space in her social calendar. I suspect there will be plenty more bar crawls in her future. Maybe Peter's, too? You never know with this kind of thing. Most marriages don't make it. It's just a matter of time." She gets up and waves to Lilly who's stopped all movement, looking at us with her thumb pressed to her lips. "Good to see you!" she cheers her way, and Lilly offers a shy smile back. Jack is too busy digging a ditch and running one of Bram's old Hot Wheels through it.

And then she is gone.

A cool breeze washes her away, and it's only then I realize I'm soaked in sweat.

My nails are embedded in my palms, a prickling of blood in their wake.

Lilly runs over. Her tiny nose is wrinkled with curiosity. "Mommy, who was that?"

"That was a very bad woman."

"Bad woman?"

"That's right, Lilly. If she ever comes near you—*run*."

I'd do the same, but it's a little hard to kill someone when they're not in your grasp.

Now, how to do it. What a wonderful project my mother has given me.

Death waits for you, Mother.

And only then will I truly live.

Twelve

Bram

That horrible day. I will never forget it. Simone called me in tears, her garbled voice panicked, afraid, riddled so thick with grief it was impossible to know what happened. She relayed there had been an accident. In the background, I could hear the shrill screams of a young girl who later I would come to find out was the sitter. Right then, not only did my world upend, but an unearthly numbness took over, brazen shock. You could have run me over with a Semi, and I wouldn't have felt a thing. My head pulsated, my heart jackhammered, but it was as if I were watching myself from the ceiling. It all unfolded in such a surreal manner. Every last second of that terrible day is ingrained indelibly in my memory. From the weather, to the way I sobbed inconsolably that night on the kitchen floor. It was all too much to believe.

The numbness hadn't had a chance to subside when

Simone died. We had just buried our children. The bitter taste of our new normal, one without the cheerful faces of our sweet angels. And I hated that everyone referred to Isla and Henry as angels. I didn't want to see them as ethereal entities floating on clouds, strumming on harps. I wanted them grounded on earth, feet to solid ground, having every day normal problems that we would detangle as a family.

My mother reminded me that they belonged to God. I didn't want them to belong to God. I wanted them to belong to me. But nonetheless, when Simone was senselessly slaughtered, the numbness thickened around me. I had become congealed in its silent bubble. Nothing was believable anymore. It was all some cruel joke playing out. Theater of the gods. I played the part of Troubled Man. It was a tragedy I wanted no part in and couldn't figure out how to escape.

But this afternoon, after stumbling upon Simone's own cryptic words, that numbness made a stark reprisal. *Anything you can do, I can do better. I can destroy anything better than you.* It was a funny quip left on her Facebook page met with cheers and emoji high fives from others. It was something she would sing to me often in jest, the second stanza in its correct form. It was cute and funny, and it was our thing. But the date, the picture of the New York skyline that went along with it, puts it at the exact time I was in fact in New York for a convention. I remember that trip specifically.

I remember that day. It was the same day I broke it off with Loretta. We were done. I was through with being Peter the Wife Cheater. I was ready to face Simone's wrath in a whole other way. I was gearing up to ask for a divorce. I had an attorney on retainer to the tune of five thousand dollars. There was an entire plan on how I would present this to Simone. It would be a weekend. I would have secured a place to stay first. I had put in applications for local rental homes—the owners of which all promptly came forward once I was the chief suspect in my wife's murder. Of course, they accused me of somehow sneaking off and killing the kids that day at the lake despite the fact records indicate I was seeing two patients that hour, both of whom spoke on my behalf. But the world wants to hear what its itching ears demand. And in the eyes of the world, I was a baby killer, a wife bludgeoner. I had done this. I was tried, convicted, drawn and quartered in the court of public opinion. Rome was burning, and for so long I wondered who really lit the flame. For so long I shouldered the blame. This was God repaying me for my sins. I was an adulterer. I deserved an implosion of my sanity. I wasn't thoughtful enough to consider the children or my wife during my philandering ways so He took them back. For so long I believed it and accepted it. Right up until this afternoon. Those cryptic words Simone posted that day reverberate in my mind: *I can destroy anything better than you.*

What did you do, Simone? What in the hell did you do?

As soon as I get home, I race up the porch and let myself in, unable to chirp out a cheery hello. The kids are running around in the backyard. I could hear their carefree voices from the driveway floating into the sky like hot air balloons. From the dining room window, I spot Ree heading this way. Her eyes are already pinned to mine. No smile.

Mace will be the first one I confide in. My mind is spinning with every damn theory. A loose cannon shooting off misery wherever I look.

"Bram?" Ree stalks in and slams the door shut behind her. Her hair is wild, and that wide-eyed look in her eyes now registers as rage. "Have you ever had drinks or dinner with other women while we've been married?" Her mouth falls open, her breathing reduced to short huffs.

My insides seize. What the hell?

"No. I save all of my dinners and drinks for you." Something warms in me as I close the gap between us and reel her in, but Ree pushes my hand away before I can seize her.

"Drinks with Astrid Montenegro. Does that ring a bell?"

A quick memory of that evening at the Thirsty Fox comes to mind. A part of me says deny it, call that cock-loving woman a lying bitch. Don't give her the pleasure of making me acknowledge something that I never wanted to happen. Don't let her make something out of nothing. But my conscience shouts *own it, do not lie*.

I shake my head as if stunned the question was peppered with innuendo, but it's purely manufactured on my part, something I think a moment like this needs. "No. I mean, she was at a bar once while I was meeting with Mace. Why? What's this about?"

Her eyes widen with grief, with a pain I've never seen in them before. "Are you having an affair?"

"What?" I'm instantly thrown for a loop. If I had suspected Ree was angry about anything, this is the last thing that would enter my mind.

The kids run in past us on their way to the kitchen, but neither of us moves, neither of us bothers to acknowledge them, our eyes locked magnetically to one another in a moment of utter despair.

"Ree? What are you saying? What's happened?" I try to get close, but she takes a full step back, her hand recoiling from my touch. "Did Astrid say something?" Stupid little bitch. She was probably setting me up the entire time. Something in my gut cinches, and I feel the need to spill it all. "She came into the office. She asked to see me only."

"Oh?" Her chest bucks with an incredulous laugh. "I bet she did." Her voice hikes in volume, deep and throaty, the way she does when she's good and pissed. The irony being that Ree has never been good and pissed at me. In fact, that's been the healing balm in this relationship. Ree and I don't argue. We disagree. This has been my first adult relationship that I didn't purposefully or otherwise royally fuck up. I liked our streak. I was hoping it would last a lifetime.

"How many times?" she insists, her voice warbling with rage. "How many times did this happen?"

"A cleaning and two small cavities," I spill the facts before her, trying desperately to remove the innuendo she's laced it with. "Three times." It takes everything I've got to keep my voice calm, but it's shaking with rage, with fear. With all of the other shit I'm going through, this shouldn't even be on the table.

The kids run back out in a flurry, and Lilly slaps me on the leg on the way into the yard in lieu of a greeting. They're so happy. So healthy. So very alive. Ree and I have it all. Can't she see that?

"I love you," I whisper. "Why are you feeling like this? I would never do anything to jeopardize our marriage."

Her lips tremble, and she never breaks her gaze, but that look of disappointment, of hurt only seems to amplify. "Why you? Why does she request you?"

A bite of heat rolls through me. I detest the direction this conversation is headed. The unspoken suggestions make me quite literally sick.

"I don't know." There. The truth. "I think she's interested in me," I practically mouth the words, but her eyes enlarge a notch, signaling that she more than understood it.

"So you admit it." She shakes her head in disbelief, and I'm right there with her.

"Look"—a small laugh chokes through me—"there's nothing going on. I don't know what she fed you—what anyone's fed you, but I wouldn't do that to you. Not to you and not to our family."

"You did it to Simone," her own voice discharges in a whisper, but those words echo through me like bells tolling for a dead man.

"What did you say?" It can't be. It's as if my life is being lived in a strange parallel to the past. The past resurfacing, resurrecting, filling its lungs with a sharp breath of my present, encroaching in on me in every direction.

Ree shakes her head, refusing to reiterate any part of

it, her feet stumbling backwards as if she were trying to get away from me.

"It's your mother, isn't it?" A mild sense of relief sweeps through me. "Of course. She's gotten into your head. Filling you with all this bullshit."

"It's not my mother. You cheated on Simone and you lied to her. You went to New York for a dental conference and you slept with some *woman*."

The world goes black. That numb feeling intensifies. Nothing feels real. Not me, not Ree, not those happy screeching children running wild outside.

A small chortling laugh escapes her, the cackle of a madwoman. "You're not denying it because you can't. My God, you did that to her. If you did it to her, what makes me think you won't do it to me?" Her eyes ride up and down my body as if the scales have fallen off and she's seeing me for the very first time. "You're a cheater?" Her body bucks with emotion. The devastation written on her face is palpable, and my heart breaks to witness it.

"I don't know what's going on. I don't know what's happening here." I take a step backwards myself. I'd like nothing more than to reverse this day, this lifetime, and do everything right the first time. "My God, I love you, Ree. You are everything Simone wasn't. You are my true wife, the one I would choose over and over, and I would never even think to betray you that way."

"Like you betrayed her." She nods as we both come to terms with this horrible, horrible truth circling the room like a serpent. "I think maybe you should go. You should pack your bags, and you should leave tonight. Go right now, Peter, and get out."

My body resonates as if I were struck on the head with a tuning fork when she said it. It felt like a gunshot to the heart when she invoked my true name.

"Go!" she thunders so loud her voice echoes in my skull long after she says it, and without protest my feet carry me upstairs.

"Shit." I rake my fingers through my hair before knocking a row of books off the dresser. "Fuck." The door to the closet sits open, and I stagger over. Here it is, my undoing part two. How in the hell did we ever get here? I flick on the lights and kick the shit out of a pile of clothes to my left, but my foot slams into something hard and the sweaters fall to the sides, revealing a box concealed underneath. I peel it open, and a small notebook catches my eye. Without thinking, I pick it up, fully expecting to find it filled with the children's scribbles, stick pictures of our nuclear family, which has indeed gone nuclear. But I'm greeted with the neat handwriting of a woman and my heart stops cold. Dated entries, familiar penmanship. Ree keeps a journal? I look to the dates one more time and freeze.

"What the hell?"

This isn't Ree's journal.

It's Simone's.

Thirteen

Twokidcircus@bex.org:

I know what you're reading.

Ree

I slept in the downstairs office. Bram left early with a soft click of the door, and even though his departing was as quiet as a whisper, it might as well have been a gunshot. Our first fight. The first big earthquake of our marriage. I had envisioned we would squabble about annoying things like who left the cap off the toothpaste. Never would I imagine it would be about a woman.

Last night I dreamed of that woman. Astrid Montenegro haunted me as proficiently as a ghost. I dreamed of her milky white teeth, the sound of her grating laughter as she looked up at my husband. I could see the lust in her eyes, feel the electric wanting of my husband oozing from her pores. This was a viral disdain brewing deep inside of me for this woman. A hatred that has ignited a rage I have tried to suppress for so very long.

The email from my old friend Twokidcircus leaves me unfazed. As shock is prone to do, it had thrown me from dissecting it further. Of course, that asshole knows what I'm reading. I'm reading the garbage they insist on sending.

No sooner do I pull back into the driveway than I glance in the direction of my sister's home and note the curtain falling back into place. I can feel my mother's evil gaze set on me like a branding iron sizzling over my flesh.

I head on inside, so many damned thoughts vying for my attention, all of them shitty. Bram is cheating. It couldn't be. He said Astrid and he were both at the bar separately and I believe him, but Simone sits on my shoulder like a devil, like a questionable angel screaming *look what he did to me!*

I set my purse on the counter and dig deep until I come up with that article I pulled out of her journal. The newspaper clipping about the children felt sacred, so I left it where I found it—but this one, the one about the potential serial killer made my skin crawl.

New York Times. A string of copycat murders leaves

police questioning whether or not there is a serial killer on the loose. Three prostitutes were strangled to death, two with wires set so tight around their necks it led to a near decapitation. In each case, the women were found to be missing the fifth digit on their left hand.

The article goes on to spotlight each of the women. All found in the city, all so very close to the midtown hotel where Bram and his paramour were staying that day Simone found them. Could she have been one of them?

The prostitute from the fundraising night comes back to me as does the prostitute from the hotel Bram was staying at last month during his conference, and as much as I want to dismiss them, I can't. It wasn't really Astrid I wanted to confront him with, but it's a hell of a lot easier to ask your husband about another woman than grill him over the death of a string of prostitutes. A part of me refuses to believe it. Bram is sweet, sensitive, loyal to a fault. And more than any of that, I can feel his love for me.

My eyes flit across the street, to that hovel my demon of a mother is holed up in. For so long she withheld real love from my sister and me. For so long we were force-fed a false adulation, praise for the illnesses we never had. She coddled her own delusions and whored us out in an effort to keep the lights on, to fund dream vacations and a short-lived stint on the talk show circuit. I've looked them up and they're still alive and well, available for anyone's viewing pleasure on YouTube. Those gullible commentators are still offering prayers for me.

I was my mother's favorite to showboat. Lena was sickly too, but for whatever reason she preferred my gauntness to hers. She sheared my hair, washed me out with pills, chemically starved me, and what food I could keep down wasn't worth much. She would have killed us as soon as she had no real use for us. We were getting older, our bodies too clunky to haul around for her heavy, panting fame.

I very much believe that death was the next prescription Dr. Van Lullen had ordered. She would have smothered us in our sleep. Scratch that. She would have researched methods to murder us in ways that were undetectable to the coroner. Something food-related, E.coli, food she smeared with her own shit. That sounds about right. She would have sent a dozen different produce products forced into a mandatory recall. She has no regard for a company's bottom line, nor her daughters' lives—not to mention her dead sister. I am still very much convinced that my aunt's death was at my mother's hands. A harbinger of things to come.

My feet carry me upstairs, past a smiling Isla and Henry, into the master bedroom, to the closet where my mother knows what I am reading, straight to the gun safe Bram brought into our marriage. He made sure I knew the code. 0307: the date of our first meeting. He knew I would never forget that. The mouth of the safe yawns open, and I give a quick glance inside to see the gun silently waiting like a dutiful guardian, the unused clip sits by its side like the forever companion it is. I shut the safe once again with a click and keep my hand on the cool metal just to feel the burn. My eyes wander behind me to the place I've stored Simone's journals. It feels sacred like a gravesite.

The sweaters I had neatly lined on top of the box sit in a jumble on the floor, and my heart kick-starts to life like a defunct motor.

"Oh my God," I whisper as I fall to my knees and yank open the box, only to discover it empty, barren of all of its treasures.

Every last journal is gone.

Fourteen

Bram

I saw two patients, and it took far more composition than I had to keep it together.

I spent the rest of the day in my office pouring over every detail of my old life as seen through my wife's eyes. Diary entries, a minutia of life most of which I don't recall. I picture myself as a seasoned politician on the stand as the prosecution pelts me with questions. I've turned into the blowhard you laugh at on TV. The Johnny One Note that says *I don't recall* on a loop. *I don't recall your honor.*

Did you sleep around on your wife?

"I plead the fifth," I say, pushing the fat stack of Simone's delusions away from me.

Who were those people? Is that truly the way she saw us? Simone stomped rose-colored glasses under her heel. She didn't wear them. This is not who we were, but she nailed the ending. She knew about Loretta. She caught me red-handed.

"God." I slam my palm down over my desk. I wish I could apologize. I wish I could take it all back. My God, Simone died with our baby in her belly.

The room seizes for a moment as I recall the coroner's findings. There was no baby inside of her the day she died. At least not according to the coroner. She must have lost it. My ridiculous, stupid, stupid affair must have riddled my poor wife with anxiety, filled her with enough toxic fury I inadvertently killed my own child.

My body bucks with grief at the thought. I knew that I was a monster. Deep down, I knew it was true, but this highlights the evidence on a whole new level.

So this is how Ree knew that I wasn't an honest man. If I cheated on Simone, the deck was already stacked against her. Astrid had very little to do with the equation. It was Simone and my screwed-up actions that led my new wife, the one who has held every piece of my heart right from the beginning, to believe the very worst in me.

Simone and I were wooden. We were off the rails before we ever began. We never should have gone as far as we did. I'd like to think we both knew that. What Simone and I had was vinegar that set our teeth on edge. What Ree and I have is a cool, refreshing drink of water. And because I couldn't keep it in my pants and walk away like a man, I buried my first marriage and my last. There won't be another after this. There is no one for me but Ree. I'll go to the grave to prove it if I have to.

My fingers swirl around the collection of my wife's thoughts, her inner workings clicking like a locomotive churning up, building speed. I have my own memories, too—the children's birthday parties, the bunny who my mother had show up one Easter and terrified poor Isla. And because Isla cried, so did Henry. The trips to the lake. The one we took in August the year before everything went to shit. Henry caught three brown trout. Isla caught five. Simone slept on the deck. It was like hauling a corpse around with us. I remember thinking that at the time. Simone hated the boat. She needed her feet on solid ground. The thought of cleaning those fish made her retch. I taught Isla and Henry the fine art of filleting. We had dinner out back over an open fire. I can still smell the smoke, feel the love we shared that day, and I drink it down as if it were a balm that had the power to heal this disease that's taken over my life—same one that extinguished theirs.

I pull over the red journal, the year before, and wince as I flip through the pages. I want to hear Simone's take once again. I blew through these pages so fast, I'm ready to take it in, soak up the good life I once had, with my precious babies I miss so damn much.

August, I flip through, no mention of the lake. I flip back to July, to June, nothing. I shoot ahead to September, and there's not a hint of us heading up there.

I rock back into my chair, trying to hone in on the dates. It was the first week of August. I'm sure of it, because we needed to get back in time for day camp. The exclusive school Isla and Henry were enrolled in had a summer program, two weeks in August. I remember that specifically. Parents bitched about it. We bitched about it. That was a lot of summertime real estate the school was asking us to part with. But the kids had to go. They wanted to see their friends, build forts, watch movies, and get their hands dirty with some good old-fashioned art.

I flip to the first week of August—right year, right week—my blood runs cold.

Peter worked late. Took the kids to the store. Drove to the aquarium. Made a boxed lunch and had a picnic in the backyard. Took the kids out for lunch before seeing a movie downtown.

"What the hell...?" I purge memory after memory—anything I can grasp, only to find that Simone seems to have rewritten history.

A rush of adrenaline hits me as I phone my brother and relay everything in three angry breathes.

"First thing's first"—his tone is unduly calm, that brotherly tone he invokes when he wants me to pull my shit together—"how did these so-called journals find themselves in your closet to begin with?"

"I don't know. Maybe I brought the box and didn't realize what was in it? No, that's not right. Hell, I"—a vision of those blood red Dutch ovens appearing one day out of the blue comes back to me—"the builders. When I sold the house, the builders sent a box of some pots and pans. Maybe they sent two boxes?"

"Why would Ree keep this from you?"

"Maybe she's embarrassed? Maybe she forgot?"

"Maybe she wrote them."

My heart stops a moment. It would be an impossible feat. "No. I think Simone knew I had an affair. I think she caught me in the city with Loretta. But the other details, like I said, she dismissed entire chunks of history and rewrote them to her liking. I don't get it."

"Maybe it was a fantasy. Maybe the new baby never existed. Regardless, I don't want you beating yourself up over it."

"Too late for that. Listen, I have to go. Ree and I—she hasn't been herself, and now I know why. I think we need to talk about this, about everything." Bile creeps up in the back of my throat just thinking about dissecting my past with my beautiful wife, pulling up the organs of something dead and rotten that is destined to stink up the present with its retched foul odor. I envision it a moment, the split belly of a pig, me trying my best to make Ree understand, and I yank up miles of gray intestines, shit squirting out everywhere, splattering the walls, our faces as we come apart at the seams. How in the hell will Ree and I survive this if Simone and I couldn't?

"There's something you need to know." Mace breathes hard into the phone. "Are you sitting?" Another healthy sigh expels from him.

"Give it to me. I don't have time for bullshit."

"I got somewhere with the people at Armadillo. It was a woman who rented the vehicle. All cash. You ready for the kicker?"

"Yes," it comes out lower than a whisper. In truth, I'm not ready for anything anymore.

"Her name was Loretta St. James."

A chill runs through me, and the room fades white as I struggle to blink my way back to the living.

"No way. It wasn't her. Loretta St. James was small, petite. She could hardly lift a hammer, let alone deliver the blows necessary to dismember Simone the way they did."

"I agree. It wasn't Loretta."

Thick silence clots the air between us as my eyes bulge at the implication.

"Who do you think killed my wife, Mace?"

"I don't know. But I've got a brand new suspect, and in the back of your mind, you do, too."

"Say it." Because God knows I don't have the balls to.

"Simone. I think she did this, Peter. She was not above teaching you a lesson."

The oxygen, all of the light seems to get sucked out of the room at once.

"You think she unraveled after the kids died? Hell, we both did. But like this? Setting up her own murder? Who in the hell would want to have their brain bashed out with a hammer?"

"I don't know. Toxicology came up with no drugs in her system, so the thought she could have self-medicated before the event is out the window. But that's not where I'm going with this." The sound of his heavy breathing eats up the line. "Peter, I think we need to come at this from another angle. We go back and talk to Kelly and find out what really happened that day."

The world bottoms out, and I'm free-falling inside this madness once again.

"Those mystery women who have sprung up dead all around you like a crop of fungi? That's no coincidence. The fact they happen to have the same finger missing as your so-called dead wife is a calling card."

"So-called," I parrot back, trying to process it all.

"The journals, Peter. You said so yourself that they don't match up to reality. Something is very fucking off here. We need to talk to her family, the Scotts, and especially her sister Meredith. I've done a little digging. No one has seen her in years."

This new angle, this new hell, has blurred the lines of reality and fantasy.

"We can't exhume Simone's body." A dull laugh rattles out of me because, my God, I seem to expertly fuck myself at every turn. "She was cremated. There's nothing left to prove that wasn't her."

"If I'm right, we won't have to prove anything. If she's out there, if her sister is, whoever the hell you've infuriated—they're gunning for you. It's showtime, baby brother, and I have a feeling they're going to keep firing bullets at your feet to watch you dance. They like the entertainment. But if I'm right, she's ready to come out of hiding, Peter."

"What does she want?" I'm not sure if I'm asking my brother or the universe at this point.

"You and everything you love, destroyed."

I hang up and sweep the sea of journals back into the trash bag I hauled them over here in to begin with. Appropriate enough, considering they just might be that. I say goodnight to the secretary on my way out into the cool evening breeze. Late spring in Percy is unseasonably warm, and normally I would be thankful, but I can't help but feel as if indeed some higher power was turning up the heat.

I jump into my car and seal myself inside, the only safe haven in an unpredictable world.

There are only a handful of options at play, only a handful of possibilities, and ironically, all of them seem impossible.

Simone is dead.

Simone is alive.

Someone who precedes Simone's death, a killer on the loose, setting me up all these years later.

No way. Impossible.

Impossible.

Possible.

Fifteen

Twokidcircus@bex.org:

Peter, Peter, pumpkin eater, had a wife and couldn't keep her. Kept her in her Percy cell and made her life a living hell. Isn't it time this living hell came to an end? I can make that happen for you.

Ree

Lena texted this morning. She said she wanted to meet for coffee, and I promptly ignored her. Oh, Lena, my precious, precious sister. My life has truly gone to hell indeed, and you are the least of my worries right now. And ironically, even the least of my problems is a bitch to contend with. The weather is overcast. All hints of spring have vanished, but the cool breeze is still infused with salt. Usually there is nothing like sea air to make me feel alive, but this numb bubble I'm living in has made even the simplest task feel as if I'm trying to accomplish it under water. Lethargy is my new friend. My appetite has dwindled. I've done research on how to successfully leave your husband. The first and only rule is drain your joint bank account. The most creative mind was Simone herself—stocking up on gift cards—a suggestion per her journals circa prior to their vanishing act. Bram has the diaries. He must. He didn't breathe a word to me about them. But in his defense, we're not speaking and he left early.

I pull into the driveway with both Lilly and Jack amped up to new heights. I swear on all that is holy, Richard E. Moss feeds them buckets of icing just before they deposit them in the pick-up line. A class action lawsuit should be issued, and knowing the snobbery and Nazi-like parent police there will be. I'll be cheering them on from the sidelines. From divorce court. From the den where I'll sequester myself while my life lies in pieces all around me. If everything is true, and Bram was simply an illusion this entire time, then I am irrevocably broken. Irreparable beyond measure. It seems cruel of the universe to plant me in a monster's womb, only to land me in front of another twenty-four years later. It's unbearable, unfathomable. A shitstorm of bad luck that seems to be interwoven right in my DNA. In the back of my mind, an angry mob of voices screams *you are not a victim*. The hell I'm not.

The kids bolt straight to the backyard, right along with Dawson barking happily in their wake, but a tiny package catches my eye at the door and I take it to the kitchen.

My name is written across the front in all capital letters, no address, no evidence it ever went through the postal system. I spin the small package in my hand looking for clues, something that suggests foul play. It's from my mother. I have no doubts about it. My gut says make a spectacle of throwing it into the trash. I know she's watching. But my heart is leaping out of my chest, my curiosity far too powerful to nullify this exchange. There is no heft, no significance whatsoever to this box of misery my mother planted on my doorstep. Throwing it away without looking inside could breed years of nightmares, years of a morbid desire to have at least taken a single peek. It's better that I look. I'll leave the box on Lena's doorstep when I'm done with it. A grown-up version of ding-dong-ditch. Lena can inspect the contents for herself when she gets home. She and my mother can work on the details of which landfill they'd like to grace it with. This is their problem. Not mine.

I pull a knife from off the counter and trace along the outer seam, popping it open, only to be met with a putrid stench. It's dark and murky, something gray, and then I see them.

My entire body seizes as I inch back, and before I can run, an impromptu paralysis hits me.

A scream locks itself in my throat. Can't breathe. Can't move. And then, like an aria, the scream releases, lusty and primal as it rises to the ceiling without my permission.

A box of fingers. Four, eight, six—hell, I can't count them, severed fingers. Curved little fingers with a crown of dried blood at the base. The one sitting on top is fresh, the fingernail painted a cheery shade of yellow. Something black and hairy sits to the side, and it takes a moment for my mind to identify it as a feather. Everything in me seizes once again. One slap of shock after the next, and I can't catch my next breath.

A feather. Black feather. *Shit, shit, shit.*

The front door loosens and jingles before opening and shutting.

"Ree?" Bram's voice fills the house right up to the rafters, and a small part of me is warmed to hear it.

A shot of adrenaline rockets through me as Bram enters the room, his eyes wide with wonder. That handsome face looks as if it's begging for mercy.

"Ree—we need to talk." He takes a step forward, and I slap my hand over the knife on the counter before lifting it between us.

"Keep away." My voice is threadbare, my chest convulsing with every breath I take.

His hands float up, his eyes wander momentarily to the box.

"Ree, it's not what you think." His voice is loud and curt, his agitation growing by the moment. "Hell, I don't know what you think, but whatever has you shaking, holding a knife like you're not afraid to use it... I think I'm being framed."

"Framed," I parrot the word back to him. Could it be? My mother in her infinite wisdom, her unbridled wickedness has taken her game to a whole new level? The knife slips from my hand. Bram doesn't miss a beat. He pulls the box over and peers inside. A guttural noise escapes him. He retches hard before jumping back.

"Shit!" He steps forward again and examines the box, scrutinizing its contents before mobilizing. Bram pulls a trash bag from under the sink, wraps the box in it, and walks it into the garage before reappearing. His eyes glazed with shock.

"Ree," he breathes my name out like a sad song. "In addition to all that sick, there was a black feather in that box. Do you know what that means?"

"That you struck again?" There's not a note of humor in my voice.

His eyes close a moment. "Brace yourself. It only goes down from here."

Sixteen

Bram

A waking nightmare. My life had been reduced to that so very long ago. There are only so many terrors a human being can undergo before the body decides to shut the shitshow down. That stark numbness I've become so familiar with has transcended into something deeper, something perhaps far more meaningful, and it's as if I'm watching all of this sublime misery from some place up in the clouds. The Peter Woodley Show. A horror flick that hasn't quite hit its climax yet. A story of misfortune embedded in sorrow and rolled in misery for good measure. It's overwritten, overdone, over-the-top, but ironically, it is not over. In fact, it might just be far from that.

In a strange ballet of what feels like choreographed moves, Ree and I head out front. The howl of a man comes from down the street as our footsteps quicken. We find ourselves in the Montenegros' backyard, only to meet up with a deluge of black feathers. A stark naked woman—Astrid herself sits stuffed in a tire swing, her neck cinched with a wire, her mouth agape, stuffed with a bloody stump with dark feathers pluming out.

Ree gags on sight, screams so loud and long she sounds like an opera singer working her vocal cords. But my eyes flit to the poor woman's left hand, bloodied as if a finger were severed, and I know which one.

Miles Montenegro lets out a low guttural cry, one after the other while I call 911 on my cell in a panic. The panic is what they expect, so I know to give it. And although the panic is indeed very fucking real, it's not entirely of the new tragedy unfolding.

"God, the kids. I'll make sure they're not watching." Ree staggers toward the house and in through the back door.

Miles falls to his knees, his face pitched toward the heavens as he shouts the word *why* over and over again. Astrid swings in the breeze, every inch of her folded body as disturbing as the next. Across the yard lie scattered pieces of that bird, that damned bird she lugged around with her everywhere she went. It looks as if it was torn apart with bare hands.

Who in the hell could do this? If Astrid saw someone so much as give a crooked look to that creature, she'd have them on a spit. Her adrenaline would have kicked in. There was probably a struggle. But that calling card. I have no doubt in my mind that a body part from that poor woman now sits in my garage in a box like some twisted trophy.

The fire department arrives on the scene, their faces white with shock, vomiting ensues. One retch inspires the next. The cops show up, and I'm shuttled out front, asked a million questions before I'm left to stagger back toward my own house. A crowd thirty deep congregates around the Montenegro home, providing an impromptu vigil.

Ree comes back out and pulls me to the side. "I called Tessa. She took the kids to her house. She's letting them spend the night. They wanted Lilly and Jack, so I sent them, too." Her voice shivers. Her body convulses as if she were having a seizure.

"It's okay." I wrap my arms around my wife, sink a kiss over the top of her beautiful head, and wonder how in the hell we will ever survive this.

Darkness falls, and the crowd dissipates. No sign of Lena or Ree's mythological mother I've yet to meet, and I was fully expecting both.

Ree lures me to the shower, undresses me robotically, undresses herself, and it's a relief, a pleasure. I would do anything to forget the last twenty-four hours, the last entire decade. She runs the water and takes me in with her, our bodies inadvertently slow dancing under a prickling of heat. Hellfire and damnation. The water's too damned hot, but it feels necessary as if it were stripping us of something horribly demonic, a past we can never escape.

Her hands cup my cheeks as she pulls me close, her skin beaded with moisture, droplets of water hanging precariously off each and every lash. Ree looks like a fantasy, a mermaid come to life with that long honey-blonde hair slicked back, her ruby lips quivering.

"Peter"—she hisses my name, my real name, and it lacerates open this wound that's been festering for so very long—"tell me right now. Did you do it? Did you kill all those women?" Her eyes search me for clues that my mouth seems unwilling to give.

"No"—it comes out curt and a touch too loud, breaking the spell for a moment—"but there are some things I need to tell you. Things that I could never have told you from the beginning."

She gives a brief nod, her gaze magnetized to mine. "There are some things I need to tell you, too."

Seventeen

Ree

For so long Bram and I coasted. We were on cruise control, autopilot. We had made it through our individual storms, come out on the other side, and we were glowing with love, frolicking through our happily ever after. Isn't that the reward you get after a bone-breaking trial saps you of all your sanity, of all your strength? You find your way home. The underdog finally gets his prize. The wicked past is decimated, and the light comes pouring into your soul. So, how in the hell is this happening again? Simple. My mother is still alive. The only way to squeeze peace out of this equation is to kill her. And after that, I must do the unthinkable. I must kill Bram.

Bram and I stare at one another while sitting on the bed like a couple of teenagers. The coroner's van rolled out of our neighborhood an hour ago. There is a box full of severed fingers in the garage, and I've been listening as

Bram steadily fills my head with things he thinks I should know about Simone. She didn't write the diaries. Correction—she fabricated their lives. These were not the right vacations. Not the right sentiments. There were pertinent verbs and nouns out of place. She may have killed her own children. She most certainly killed those hookers *Peter* did not have an affair with. She killed Loretta, a woman Peter did care for at one time, but he was very, very confused. In his right mind, with the right wife—me—that would never have happened. She killed the prostitute I found, the woman from the fundraiser, and baited me toward her. She killed Astrid. A staggering body count, considering Simone has supposedly killed from beyond the grave. The kicker, of course, is that Simone is not dead. She could not be dead. There is no way of telling who was killed because Peter and his former in-laws mutually decided to have her cremated, and rightly so since there was hardly anything left of her head.

As if perfectly timed, Bram's brother calls and drops a bombshell. Meredith, Simone's sister, has not been seen since before Simone's murder.

"It was her." Bram nods into this lunacy.

"What about dental records? Even siblings have different teeth. Surely the coroner—"

"Her teeth were obliterated. We went off DNA and matched them to her parents."

My heart drums wildly. A blast of anxiety rockets through me, throws me off balance and makes the room feel as if it's starting to spin.

"Ree"—he reaches over and picks up my hand, rubbing small circles over my palm like he did when we first met—"I love you. I swear, I would never lie to you."

I pluck my hand away as if pulling it from the flames. "You just keep things from me. You painted your relationship with Simone as perfect. You never demonized her until now. Why now?"

His eyes bulge with a strangulating stare. "Because we have a box of human digits smelling up the garage. Why would I send those to myself? To *you*?"

I shake my head, my gaze flitting through the north wall to that demonic place where my mother's sick mind resides.

"She's been here. She's been in the yard. Lena probably let her in the house. Wherever you've had them hidden, she's known about them for months." My mother must have hit her zenith once she found that box of severed human remains. It was right up her twisted alley. "I've been getting these emails."

"What emails?" His voice is curt, a little too loud for my liking.

"They have nothing to do with it. Not really," I say, inching back on the bed. For the first time since we've met, I want to get away from this man, this enigma who I not only thought I knew but who I thought I understood on a deep, intimate level. It was all a joke to him. I was the easy wife, so gullible, very willing to buy whatever he was peddling.

I ate my way through his bucket of bullshit and asked for more. Thank you, Bram. May I have another?

Even his name is a lie. My children are born from this half-truth. My God, we're going to have to get away, far away from Percy, and this time there will be no Lena, no old Bram, no support whatsoever to help me navigate my way through this difficult, difficult world. And worse than that, I'll have spent my life looking over my shoulder for Bram of all people. My own husband, the murdering monster. But that's not happening. That is simply not where this is headed. It's a good plan C or D, but it's not my first choice.

No. Bram is proving to be wily, but I will prove to be far more deceptive. I have always believed that if necessary I could kill someone. If absolutely necessary—if I truly put my mind to it, I can get away with it, too. None of this *I'm a woman with a broken mind* defense either. This will have to be a bona fide murder, just not by my hands. I need someone with a history of violence and, lucky for me, I have my mother. What a strange victory to rid the world of my mother—*and* place the blame of my husband's own unfortunate demise on her shoulders. And if Lena dares get in my way, she will have to go, too.

"Ree"—he pulls me back into the room with the firm command of his voice—"what emails?"

"My mother sent them."

I pull my phone forward and show him every last one.

Bram's features mold into a permanent look of disdain.

"It's not fair." His chest bucks. "It's not fair that you have to bear the burden of your cold-hearted mother, and I have to bear the burden of a psycho bitch ex-wife."

"*Wife*," I correct. "You never divorced. If she's alive, she still belongs to you."

His gaze penetrates mine. It says *please believe me. I would never lie to you. I would die for you.*

Yes, Peter, Bram, whoever you are.

You will most assuredly die for me.

It's time to put a call in to my mother—and then do what I must do.

Eighteen

Bram

Hello, Bram. Do you want to play a game?

I stare down at the text from a number I don't recognize an inordinate amount of time before putting a call to my brother and relay the new—the old nightmare blooming before me.

"What the hell?" Mace pants into the phone as if he ran a mile to get there. "Get Ree and the kids, and take off for the night. Somebody is fucking with you. Hell, it could be her, and, if it is, she's stalking you."

"The kids are gone for the night. They're staying with friends. Ree looks as if she's about to turn me in. Simone has done a fantastic job of infiltrating her mind. Dead or alive, she's still got it."

"I hear that. Give me the number. I'm going to try to get a read on where she is."

"How the hell are you going to do that?"

"I might just call and ask. She's the one who said she's up for a game. I say we give her one."

I send Mace the number and get off the phone before heading back inside the house to be with Ree. To comfort Ree. To tell her there is yet another sinister plot twist that's guaranteed to keep us up at night. She's not in the kitchen, the dining room, or the living room.

"Ree?" I call out just as she comes bounding down the stairs, a wild look in her eyes, her jacket and shoes on, a purse slung over her shoulder. "Where are you going?"

Her glassy eyes settle over mine. Ree looks chemically altered, slightly deranged, stoned. "It's time you met my mother." She holds her hand out to me. "Come, Peter. She would love to meet you."

I have seen my wife through every measure of pain, emotional—especially when we spoke of Isla and Henry, physical—giving birth to our own children, and yet this glazed look she's wearing like a mask, I don't recognize it at all. It's as if she's fractured. This is it. Peter Woodley strikes again. I've killed her on the inside where it truly counts, and I can only pray she recovers.

"I don't think it's a good idea," I say, trying to steer her to the sofa, but she jerks my hand away.

"I do." Her gaze burns like fire over me, her voice curt and angry. "You will love her. The two of you have so very much in common." She ushers us out the door without bothering to shut it, and I glance back at the open mouth, the burst of light beaconing into the night that lets the rest of the neighborhood know there is something amiss. But on a night like tonight. Tonight, of all nights, it might not register a wayward blink.

Lena's home is dark, save for the soft flicker of light emanating from the television in the living room. I haven't been a regular guest at Lena's rental the way Ree has, but I've been over enough to know the layout, to realize where the exits are in the event I need to escape the madness, and something tells me I will.

My phone buzzes in my pocket, and I stop in the middle of the street to fish it out. Ree goes on ahead and waits by Lena's walkway. Ree would never intentionally put herself in harm's way. That's exactly what I love about her. Not only is she safe, but she prefers to keep herself that way. Her fierce level of self-preservation is the only reason she's with us today. And the monster behind those walls is the reason she almost didn't make it.

I glance at the screen. It's a text from Mace. **I know in general where she or whoever is at. Get the hell out of Percy and do it tonight. If you don't assure me you're leaving, I'm calling the police.**

"Shit," I mutter as a pair of headlights speed this way, and I jog over to safety, to Ree who's holding herself, shivering. I grip her by the arms and pull her in close. "We can't do this right now. We need to leave. We're in danger. We need to get the kids and leave Percy right now."

"No!" Her voice riots into the night with a level of insanity in it that I've never heard before. "We stay." Her breathing is ragged as plumes of white fog billow from her mouth. "My mother has been waiting for this moment, and I'm not about to deny her. You owe me that, Peter. You owe me so much more than you'll ever realize."

My phone bleats with a text once again, and I glance down. Same mysterious number. Same number Mace warned me about. Just four words.

Let the games begin.

My blood runs cold as I give a quick glance around at the vicinity. It's as if I can feel them—feel her watching me, watching us, and for that reason alone I head to the door.

Ree gives a low and furtive knock. "Open up, Mother." She does her best to keep her voice even-tempered as not to attract any more attention than our neighborhood has already called to itself tonight. "Lena? It's me. I have to talk to you."

A rustle emits from the other side. The sound of footfalls heads in this direction as ominous as steel drums with the skin pulled tight. The door gives a quick jiggle, and the lock releases with a snap.

Ree looks up at me from under her lashes just like that first day we met, and I can't help but wonder if this will be our last.

"Come inside, Peter. I can't wait for you to meet Mommy."

Nineteen

Ree

When I was a child, my mother turned to me one night and whispered *everybody hates you*. It was matter-of-fact, a hard lesson that a mother had to teach her child, a cold-hearted truth that I needed to swallow down like the syrup she so often poured down my throat.

Lena hadn't heard it, and I was thankful for that, embarrassed that we had brought so much scorn on our young selves without trying. My mother never quantified her statement, but left me alone to fill in the blanks. And my mind worked nonstop listing all of the obvious reasons a cruel world would look to me with such disdain.

Looking back, as an adult, as someone who has absorbed copious amounts of self-help books, as someone who has listened to psychologists and psychiatrists alike as they tried to untangle the verbal knot my mother employed, I can see now that it was yet another method she employed to mentally restrain me.

But tonight, I'm here to return the favor. Upon her dying breath, I want her to realize that the world never hated me. It was her all along. There are not a lot of justifications for murder. There are not a lot of reasons that I would willingly go to prison for—that is, if I'm caught—but my mother has built up a damned good argument, along with a body count, and she would be worth the risk. I don't know who killed Peter's first wife. I do not know who killed those poor women littering his past. But I have no doubt my mother has latched onto the madness, her last desperate attempt to fuck with my mind—to kill me by taking away my husband.

And Peter. What can be said about Peter other than the fact he does not look innocent. Is it a coincidence that I left one feral psychopath, only to fall into the arms of another? In truth, I can't sort any of it out. All I know is that I need to excise the demons from my life. Both the past and the present must go in hopes that the children and I can have a safer tomorrow.

The porch light ignites as the door yawns open, and Lena stands there hugging her bathrobe.

"What's going on?" Her voice is groggy. Lena is an early riser in order to open the Blue Chandelier.

I push my way past her, dragging Peter in beside me. *Bram.* I can't even bring myself to go along with the Bram farce anymore.

"Where is she?"

A set of soft footsteps heads this way from the hall, and Lena crosses the room just as my mother emerges. Her dark hair is damp from the shower, her skin vacant of the theatrical pancake makeup she's come to adorn her face with.

"Well, look who's here." Her lips curve unnaturally in a vertical manner, something I've only seen cartoon villains pull off. It looks downright menacing. "So, you've finally brought the hubby."

"Did you manage to wash all the blood off?" My voice carries across the room like an apparition streaming from my mouth with an agenda of its own. I'm not sure I meant to hit the highlights so soon, but my adrenaline keeps hiking higher to far more frightening levels than ever before.

"*Ree*." Peter tries to pull me back a notch, but I wrangle myself free.

"I want to know." I shrug over at the two of them huddled at the base of the hall as if they thought running were an option. "Did you take pleasure in killing Astrid? Did it thrill you when you dismembered that bird and jammed it down her throat?"

Lena shakes her head as she slowly backs away from my mother. "Did you do this? Is that why you were gone so long this afternoon?"

Our mother balks at the thought, looking to my sister as if she lost her mind. Forever the actress. She has honed her chops. Nearly two decades' worth of performances. She slayed them night after night in preparation for the literal slayings. It was all leading up to death. I should have seen it coming.

"The emails weren't enough." I take a step away from Peter and pull the gun from my purse, pointing it in his direction. "Get over there. It's time for a formal introduction." I wave the gun as his hands ride up naturally, his wide eyes focused right over the barrel.

"Ree." His voice drops to its lower octave.

"Mother"—my voice trembles with rage—"you have always wanted to meet my husband. You have about thirty seconds left of your disgusting life. Say hello."

Her pie hole opens—the black maw of her mouth that devoured me right along with the thousands of empty calories she spent during my childhood shoveling into her face. She wouldn't let Lena or me have a single bite, so she ate our share, ate for us. She ate our souls in the process.

"What emails, Ree?" Her eyes glint in this dim light like a coin underwater as the sun passes it by. Forever doomed, sealed off from the world and its purpose.

A dark laugh gurgles in my chest, and I suddenly feel alive, far more in this world than I have ever felt before. "You don't have to play dumb, but if that's how you insist to leave this world, with a lie on your lips, then so be it."

"*Lena*," my mother barks. "Are you going to stand there and let her tarnish my good name?"

Lena shakes her head, her body shaking as she looks to her. "Pull the trigger."

And I do.

Twenty

Bram

"*Ree*," my voice rings out far louder than the silencer allowed on the Glock as I drop to my knees as Cordelia lies dying. Chest wound, right side. Probably hit a lung.

Her body twitches, her lids fluttering as she struggles to fight it. But blood pools rapidly around her. It's the end for her, and she knows it.

I pluck my cell phone out of my back pocket, and Lena kicks it out of my hand.

"Shit." I look up at a frail looking woman, eyes alive with fire. I hadn't seen Lena up close in weeks. She looks like half the woman she was, her face unnaturally pale like a creature who has never seen the light. "Lena, call 911. We can fix this." I look to my wife, her body shaking aggressively, the gun still waving in my direction. Her teeth are clenched as if she were biting down on an invisible bit and for the life of her she can't seem to let go.

I would have gotten her help. I will *get* her help. If only I had known her trauma went soul deep. Hell, I knew it. I just pretended it was over, the same way I pretended my past was over.

"I did it, Mother." Lena laughs the cackle of a madwoman. "I sent those texts to Ree because I knew she would blame you for it."

"Lena?" Ree's voice is as fragile as her state of mind.

The dying woman looks up at her older daughter, her tongue protruding as she shudders and bucks.

But her sister persists. "When you contacted me, and said you were going to be a part of our lives whether we liked it or not, I knew I only had one choice to make. I never wanted you here. Never in God's name did I want you as a part of our lives. The hell I was going to let you become the quintessential grandmother to Lilly and Jack." She looks to Ree. "I knew you would shut her out. I knew you would hold her at bay. I was willing to sacrifice what we have for a little while to get us where we needed to be." She points hard at the pool of blood forming around her mother's torso. "I was going to do it." Lena shakes her head. "You didn't have to kill her. I was going to take care of everything. I wanted her gone forever, Ree. I wanted it more than you did."

"Le-*na*," Cordelia croaks her daughter's name out in a broken whisper.

Lena shakes her head at the old woman. "You sold my body to greasy old men. You let them into our home to have their way with me. I was too weak to defend myself, but it was only a matter of time. I knew I wasn't going after them. They were nameless, faceless bastards who meant nothing to me. Junkies and perverts, the scum you dredged from the forbidden dangerous alleyways."

"*No.*" Ree retches as if she might vomit.

"Yes." Lena nods over at her. "I begged her not to use you, too. I volunteered to take on whatever load she brought home for you, Ree. I loved you more than I loved myself. And I never thought I'd share this with you. But I need her to know that I wanted to kill her first."

"Oh God." Ree bucks, her entire body convulsing as she begins to sob. The gun dances in her hands like it's trying to fly away.

"You killed Lena!" Ree shouts as Cordelia's listless eyes shift slowly her way. "You killed those women. You never deserved a breath on this earth."

Lena looks to me. "And now we are going to excise the second demon from our life."

A second gunshot flits through the air and Lena falls to the floor. Head shot. Dead on contact.

Shit.

I turn back, but it's not Ree who has my attention.

Holy hell.

This is it.

Twenty-One

Ree

"Lena?" My voice sounds disembodied, otherworldly as I glance to the gun still wavering in my hand. "Did it go off? Did I kill her?"

"I killed her," a voice drones from behind, and I turn just in time to see a gun pointed at me, a steady hand, an unfamiliar redhead standing with her feet in a defiant stance. "You're going to live, Ree. Put the gun down."

"Ree," Bram barks. "*Shoot*."

I look to him as he rises to his feet, his hands right back in the air.

"Hello, Simone." Bram's voice is strangled, his eyes focused right over hers, and my heart detonates in my chest over and over, my adrenaline spiking anew as if it had never even crested this evening.

"Simone," her name expires from me like a collapsing tire. "You killed Lena." I take a stumbling step toward what's left of my sister. Her hair is clotted with blood, her face torn open on the right, her teeth splayed out unnaturally.

A horrible wailing sound rips from my throat.

"Ree!" Peter roars, and I turn to Simone, my gun shifting toward her.

Her face, her beautiful face, she looks exactly how she did in those pictures. I had worshipped her for so long, admired her from afar, felt sorry for her, grieved her as if she were my own blood.

Her lips turn upward as if flirting with a wicked grin. "You're going to kill Bram." Her green eyes pin to mine, her steady aim sending my own limbs bucking all the more.

"*Shoot her*," Peter riots so loud the windows reverberate.

"Don't do it." Simone's voice wavers with anger. I can feel the rage emanating off her like a heat from a radiator. "You'll miss and I'll be forced to kill you. I don't want to do it, but just know when you pull that trigger it's you who will die."

"She's lying." Peter takes a careful step forward, and Simone twitches the gun his way.

"You're going to die, Peter. You will meet your maker. You will live forever with Isla and Henry."

My eyes widen in disbelief. What has happened? Was Bram right all along? This monster had laced my mind against him. I was nothing more than another one of her pawns.

"All of this because he had an affair." I shake my head in disbelief. "Then it's true. You killed your children. Did you have the third? Or did you kill it, too?"

Simone lets out a barking laugh, her cackle unnaturally dark. "I have Peter, my Peter." Her eyes flit to Bram. "He is strong and beautiful and smart, and you will never know him. You could have, though. We could have had it all, but you had no desire to love me. You were going to leave and take my babies. I gave you everything!" Her voice thunders as she looks right at him. "And you destroyed it all for a cheap fuck. Divorcing you would have been too easy. You didn't deserve my children or me. I watched you once I was gone. I lived where you lived." That smile reprises itself on her lips as she glances my way. "I was right there out in the open, dancing through life, laughing at how easy it all was."

"And then he met me." My voice trembles lower than a whisper. "You left us alone. You watched us build a family."

"Yes." She nods, incredulous, as if there was no other way. "You had one boy, one girl, and I was hoping it would be so. I thought of killing the kids, waiting until they were as old as Isla and Henry were when Peter killed them." She glances his way. "You did, Peter. When you killed our marriage, you killed all of us. My hands were your hands the day I held them under. Do you realize how disciplined you need to be to hold two children fighting for their life underwater? I only had minutes before Kelly finished her blubbering conversation. It was the only time in my life I was thankful for teen angst. I made it look as if I were trying to save them and, of course, she believed me. The world believes me. No one believed you, though, Peter— did they? You don't get to keep your horny girlfriend and get the kids on weekends. You don't win because you cheated. You don't get to rid yourself of me and the so-called misery I inflicted on you. I loved you the only way I knew how. I warned you the night we were married." She nods his way. "What did I tell you? Pop quiz. Pass and I might make it quick for you."

Peter closes his eyes. His chest bucks a moment. "You said, 'you may never leave me.'"

"And you left. Emotionally first and then physically. You brought home her filth and defiled our bed with it. You thought you could do it again and again and your stupid wifey would be none the wiser." She scoffs my way. "All you are, Ree, is just another fling I've allowed my husband to have. When he met you, when you built your family, I knew the perfect revenge would come in time. Make Peter suffer a little bit more, let him live with the uncertainty of what might come next, just like I did. Lilly and Jack are just about the same age that Isla and Henry were when they died. Newsflash, Ree, your fake family has reached its expiration date." She looks to Peter, and her lips curl unnaturally on the sides. "Your wife, who you love so very much, is going to kill you. My hands are clean. I am a living, breathing ghost in this world, new identity, great job, great new man in my life. Peter and I are doing just fine. Ree will go to prison, unfortunately." She manufactures a frown my way, and I try my best to steady the gun her way. "Ah-ah!

Remember, Ree, you pull the trigger, you die, Peter dies. Murder-suicide, such a bad romance. At least in prison, you might see your children's faces again."

"Ree." Peter's voice shakes. "She's wearing a vest. You'll have to hit her head or shoot the gun out of her hands. Look at me, Ree. I want you to look right at me. I have to tell you something important. Simone, you're going to want to hear this, too. There's—"

A gunshot goes off behind me, the same stifling whistling sound the silencer made, and Simone's head explodes like a piñata.

Oh God. The blood.

It's everywhere.

So much blood.

The world goes gray as I fall softly to the floor.

Twenty-Two

Bram

As soon as I saw Mace lurking outside the window, gun drawn, I knew I had to think fast. It was him I was alerting to Simone's Kevlar vest, him I was barking out orders to. As he entered the room, I knew I needed to keep command of both Ree and Simone's attention.

"Call the police," I say as I roll my sleeve over my hand and take the gun from Ree's listless hand. I wipe down the handle before sidestepping over to Simone and rubbing her fingers all over it, making it look like a struggle ensued before depositing it to the floor.

"Mason." I pull my brother to the side, his wild eyes meeting up with mine. "It's time to get our stories straight."

No sooner do Mace and I hash it out than a squad car pulls up in front of the house with flashing lights. Soon, the entire room is determined a crime scene. The medics give

Ree oxygen and roll her out on a gurney as she extends her hand to mine.

"Bram." Her voice breaks as she calls to me, calling me by the only name she has ever truly known me by.

I lean over and kiss her firmly on the lips. "I'll be with you as soon as I can."

"Bram." Her voice is threadbare as she sheds silent tears. "I love you."

"I know. I love you more than life, Ree. And I mean the hell out of it."

There are moments in your life when you feel blessed beyond measure. Moments when you realize that the proverbial sun is shining warm on your back, and the dark, cold night of the soul is over. For as long as I have known Simone, for as long as I thought she was out of my life for good, I felt unsettled, my bones ached with misery, they resounded her name, and I never understood why until now. She was here, lurking in the corners of my life, orchestrating her next murderous move. There was never any leaving her. I understood it then, just the way I do now. I was trapped, bound by her insanity. We both were.

The ambulance roars out with Ree inside, with my very heart riding in the back.

Mace and I are taken downtown for questioning.

They ask for the truth, and we give it to them.

Just the way we rehearsed.

Twenty-Three

Ree

We cremated my sister and my mother—scattered their ashes at opposite ends of the boat Bram hired to take us out for the day. We left the kids with Tessa. They know Lena is gone. They never understood their grandmother, and I'm thankful they don't know enough to ask—yet, I suppose.

Bram pops a bottle of fine champagne, expensive, from France as the captain cruises us back to port. I had jokingly suggested it, a small way to celebrate my sister's beautiful but all too brief existence and, of course, Bram didn't hesitate to oblige me.

"To life." Bram's ocean blue eyes rival the Pacific with their majestic beauty.

"To life and life unstoppable," I counter.

Peter Junior is spending the day with his uncle Mason. He looks so much like Henry did in those pictures.

In a way, it's as if Peter got a piece of Henry back, too. Little Peter loves Lilly and Jack, and both Lilly and Jack adore their new older brother.

Tessa helped us find a top-notch therapist who is working to gently untangle the knot our family had become.

We are powering through this with love, with the fuel of our newfound vindication, with the idea that we can and we will persevere. After all, it was the storms of life that thrust us together right from the beginning—with a little help from Simone, of course. There was no chance meeting that first day at the bar. That shock of red hair Simone wore like a bad wig, I remember it distinctly. I was taking yoga downtown twice a week and she made it a practice to stand next to me, her face the same, but her eyes ringed heavy with kohl. It was her I was supposed to meet at the bar that day I met Bram. She was luring me there. I can see that now. Orchestrating our every move from afar and we happily played into her hands. It never occurred to me until years later when I forced myself to look at pictures of Simone, the sweet understated face, hair as pale as straw that she could have been one in the same. And why would I? My mind doesn't work that way, and I'm thankful for it.

"Why do you think she chose me?" I nestle into my husband's arms, and he is my husband. Bram and I went to the courthouse and made it official. Took the kids to dinner afterwards.

"I have no doubt she handpicked you. She took her time looking for just the woman she wanted to pair me with. Simone knew me well. She knew there would be an instant attraction. And she knew our brokenness would solder us to one another. She knew we would be perfect together. I think she was hoping I'd settle down, build a family. It's no fun to pick apart someone's world if they have nothing to live for, nothing to lose."

My blood runs cold a moment. "I guess in the end she was right." I wrap my arms around my gorgeous husband. "We are perfect together."

He presses a warm kiss to my lips, his lids hooded low as he pulls away. "To perfection." He lifts his glass once again before draining it. "You're not drinking." His brows hood for a moment as he lands his glass to the table next to us.

"I can't." My gaze pins over his. "It's not good for the baby."

"The baby?" His face smooths out. Every worry line dissipates as his eyes widen with relief, with joy. Bram pulls me in tight, his chest bucking against mine as tears and laughter hit him at once. "We are expanding our family. I love you so much, Ree. Thank you for this." He blesses me with another kiss, oven-heated and full of desire, full of hope.

Our lives hadn't truly started, our family never truly lifting off the ground until Simone died. She was the puppet master, the false god in the wings directing our steps, casting a sun far too hot over our weary heads, so hot it incinerated her own soul to the ground. But we can breathe now. We can see the light.

Lena and my mother are both gone, two very different women who should never even be spoken of in the very same sentence. But I'd like to think in the end, my mother had truly believed she'd changed, that she wanted something real.

Lena never abandoned me like I had thought once my mother arrived. In fact, it was the opposite. It was Lena trying to fix things, taking a twisted page from my mother's dark book, the aftermath from which we never recovered. Lena was too busy setting up my mother, setting my teeth on edge. She was willing to put our relationship on hold. I don't know what she thought would happen, but I know that she would have killed our mother, perhaps was too afraid I would fall for the new version of the demon that raised us. And I might have. The emails were a necessary evil. She needed to remind me in a clever manner that my mother was still herself. And whether she was or not, I will never know.

Simone's DNA was discovered on Astrid's shoe. A single hair—just enough for us to realize it was truly Simone's insanity that racked up the body count. In fact, Erwin Wilson is in the process of being released because of it—because of everything brought to light. The girl at the hotel, the girl at the fundraiser. Simone was responsible for them all. And her sister, Meredith. Her parents mourned her first when they learned of the devastating news. Her father called and personally apologized to me. He wanted me to understand that Simone saw people as possessions right from the beginning. It was a cute quirk at first, something he and his wife were sure she'd grow out of. But she didn't. She never would.

Bram and I head home. We share the news with the kids, and we all go out to dinner to celebrate this new addition to our family.

Summer has crested, and we're packing our things, moving from Percy Bay.

It was a good place. It filled a need we hadn't even known we had. It forged us into who we were destined to be all along.

A true family.

Acknowledgements

Thank you for reading THE FIRST WIFE'S SECRET. I hope you're willing to join me on my next adventure. I had a lot of fun peeling back the layers of Ree and Bram, and I hope you did, too.

Big thank you to Ashley Marie Daniels, Shay Rivera, and Lisa Markson for being my early readers and making this book sparkle and shine.

Thank you to Kathryn Jacoby for proofreading. I adore you and your amazing kids.

A special thank you to Jodie Tarleton, Kaila Eileen Turingan-Ramos and Donna Rich for your proofreading services as well.

And to the amazing Paige Maroney Smith, without whom this book wouldn't nearly be as shiny—thank you from the bottom of my heart.

And last, but never least, thank you to Him who sits on the throne. Worthy is the Lamb! Glory and honor and power are yours. I owe you everything.

About the Author

Addison Moore is a *New York Times*, *USA Today*, and *Wall Street Journal* bestselling author who writes contemporary and paranormal romance. Her work has been featured in Cosmopolitan Magazine. Previously she worked as a therapist on a locked psychiatric unit for nearly a decade. She resides on the West Coast with her husband, four wonderful children, and two dogs where she eats too much chocolate and stays up way too late. When she's not writing, she's reading.

Feel free to visit her at:

Website: www.addisonmoore.com
Facebook: Addison Moore Author
Twitter: @AddisonMoore
Instagram: @AuthorAddisonMoore
http://addisonmoorewrites.blogspot.com

Made in the USA
Middletown, DE
05 November 2023